October 1998

For Judy —
with warmest wishes from
Katherine Kirkpatrick

Trouble's Daughter

The Story of Susanna Hutchinson, Indian Captive

KATHERINE KIRKPATRICK

DELACORTE PRESS

To my writers' group
and
to three teachers of the heart—
Marianne Fuenmayor,
Madeleine L'Engle,
and Susan Ji-on Postal

Published by
DELACORTE PRESS
BANTAM DOUBLEDAY DELL PUBLISHING GROUP, INC.
1540 Broadway
New York, New York 10036

Library of Congress Cataloging-in-Publication Data
Kirkpatrick, Katherine.
    Trouble's daughter : the story of Susanna Hutchinson, Indian captive / Katherine Kirkpatrick.
        p.   cm.
    Includes bibliographical references.
    Summary: When her family is massacred by Lenape Indians in 1643, nine-year-old Susanna, daughter of Anne Hutchinson, is captured and raised as a Lenape.
    ISBN 0-385-32600-9
    1. Hutchinson, Susanna, b. 1633—Juvenile fiction.
[1. Hutchinson, Susanna, b. 1633—Fiction.   2. Indian captivities—Fiction.   3. Delaware Indians—Fiction.   4. Indians of North America—New York (State)—Fiction.   5. New York (State)—History—Colonial period, ca. 1600–1775—Fiction.]   I. Title.
PZ7.K6354Tr   1998
[Fic]—dc21   98-6030
                                                                                    CIP
                                                                                    AC

The text of this book is set in 12-point Minion.
Book design by Semadar Megged
Manufactured in the United States of America
October 1998
10   9   8   7   6   5   4   3   2   1
BVG

Trouble's Daughter

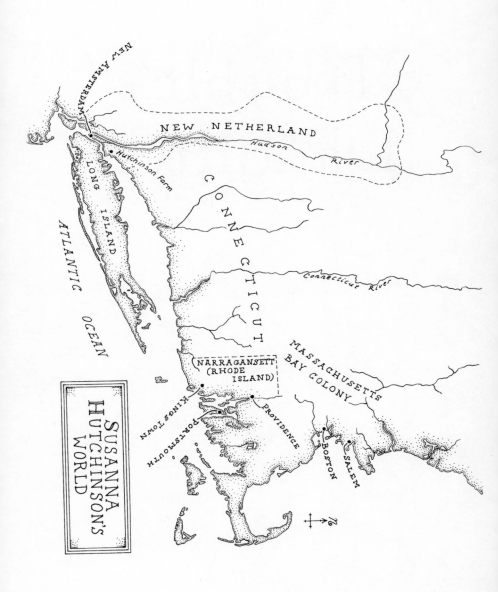

NEW AMSTERDAM

NEW NETHERLAND

Hudson River

Hutchinson Farm

LONG ISLAND

ATLANTIC OCEAN

CONNECTICUT

Connecticut River

MASSACHUSETTS BAY COLONY

NARRAGANSETT
(RHODE
ISLAND)

KINGSTOWN

PORTSMOUTH

PROVIDENCE

BOSTON

SALEM

SUSANNA
HUTCHINSON'S
WORLD

LENAPE-HAW-KING
PLACE OF THE PEOPLE
(Land of the Lenape)

Hutchinson farm

MUS-KAY-KWEE-MING
Place of Swamp
Huckleberries

UK-WA-NU-MAY-WUNG
Place Where They Fish with Nets

TAH-KOH-EE-MU-NU-PEK
Turtle Pond

MUS-KAY-KUNG
Place Where
There Is
a Swamp

HA-KEE-HA-KUN
Cornfield

CHEEK-WU-LU-LEE-SHING
Place of Seashells

KTU-MÄK-SU-WA-KING
Pitiful Place
(Burial Ground)

EK-HUS-SING
Place of Clams

LAP-HA-WAH-KING
Place of
Stringing Beads
Village

NEE-SHA-MU-NA-TAY
Two Islands

KWEE-KWEENG-HA-KING
Place Where There Are Ducks

KA-AK-HA-KING
Place of Pigeons

AHEE-MEE-HA-KING
Geese Land

SU-KA-NAH-KING
Black Treetop Place

KITA-HEEKUN
Ocean (Long Island Sound)

Som-Kway's Family Tree

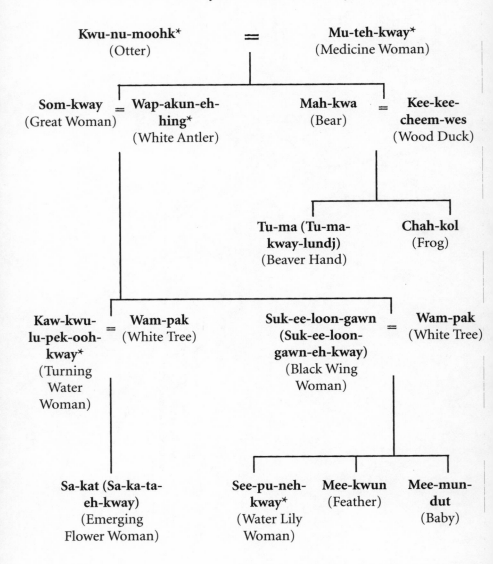

Kwu-nu-moohk* (Otter) **=** Mu-teh-kway* (Medicine Woman)

Som-kway (Great Woman) **=** Wap-akun-eh-hing* (White Antler)

Mah-kwa (Bear) **=** Kee-kee-cheem-wes (Wood Duck)

Tu-ma (Tu-ma-kway-lundj) (Beaver Hand)

Chah-kol (Frog)

Kaw-kwu-lu-pek-ooh-kway* (Turning Water Woman) **=** Wam-pak (White Tree)

Suk-ee-loon-gawn (Suk-ee-loon-gawn-eh-kway) (Black Wing Woman) **=** Wam-pak (White Tree)

Sa-kat (Sa-ka-ta-eh-kway) (Emerging Flower Woman)

See-pu-neh-kway* (Water Lily Woman)

Mee-kwun (Feather)

Mee-mun-dut (Baby)

* deceased at beginning of book

The Children of
Anne Marbury Hutchinson (1591-1643)
and William Hutchinson* (1586-1642)

Edward   1613–1675   =   Catherine Hamby

Susanna*   1614–1630, died in England

Richard   1615–date of death unknown

Faith   1617–1651 or 1652   =   Thomas Savage

Bridget   1618–before 1698   =   John Sanford

Francis   1620–1643, Indian attack

Elizabeth*   1622–1630, died in England

William*   1623–date of death unknown,
died young in England

Samuel   1624–date of death unknown

Anne (Annie)   1627–1643, Indian attack   =   William Collins

Mary   1628–1643, Indian attack

Katherine   (Kate) 1630–1643, Indian attack

William   1631–1643, Indian attack

Susanna   1633–before 1713   =   John Cole

Zuriel   1636–1643, Indian attack

Stillborn baby*   1638

* deceased at beginning of book

The Warning

THE DOGS WERE THE FIRST TO SENSE TROUBLE.

Most of the family were bringing in greens from the garden, but my sister Kate and I were husking corn outside the open door. I was careful not to get corn silk on my apron and my new blue woolen dress. Mother was inside trimming six-year-old Zuriel's brown curls. The dogs raced out of the barn and barked at two strange men approaching the fence of our enclosure.

Indians! Indians had never come to our house before.

My brother-in-law Will tied up the dogs; then he opened our gate. The Indians walked toward our house, each carrying one large bluefish. They were full-grown men with bare chests and red and black paint smeared on their faces. The taller one had a long, gaunt face and a picture of a snake inked into his forehead. The other had a bone ornament in his nose. Their heads were bald and shiny, except for a long tuft of hair on top, tied up with a few feathers. My breathing quickened. "Susanna. Kate. Come inside!" Mother called. She did not seem afraid.

Will extended his hand, but the Indians did not respond. Mother showed them into the house, where the bluefish dripped a thin trail of blood and muddy water. Kate and I followed. Zuriel clung to my leg. The Indians' dark eyes scanned the cooking pots hanging from a crane over the fire; the stools, benches, and beds; the butter churn, the spinning wheel, the basket of flax, the family's Bible.

The tall one made a startling noise like a deep cough. He set the fish down on the table.

Mother said, "A gift! We are grateful."

Will encouraged the men to sit on our benches. Mother told me, "Susanna, fetch some bread for our guests." She put some butter on it and they ate hungrily.

"I'm sorry I've no sweet puddings to give you," she continued. "I think you would like them, but one must make do in the wilderness."

I was sure that Mother's words made no sense to them. *Mother, stop,* I thought.

Mother tried to smile, but she was pale. The Indians continued to look around the room. They smelled of fish and grease, wet skins, and smoke.

We sat in silence until Mother said, "There have been many misunderstandings between the Indians and the colonists. People by nature seem to want to divide the world into the blessed and the wretched, the good and the evil."

My sister Annie, her face blank, came from the garden and stood near the doorway beside her husband, Will.

The Indians licked up the last of our bread and stood up. The tall one with the snake on his forehead took a step toward me. His fingers snatched at my long red hair. I drew back and looked at my feet as they left.

"They were curious about your hair, Susanna," Mother said.

"You should have kept them away from me!"

"I know they frightened you. I'm sorry. They meant no harm. Don't you see that they liked you? Perhaps they've never seen red hair before."

"A curious visit," Will said.

I gathered my hair in back of me. What was that smell? Strange. Sharp. It was the odor of the Indians, left behind in our home.

• • •

That night I dreamed I was running through the fields, screaming. Someone called, "Susanna!" I woke with a start. My heart was pounding. In the dark I reached out for my rag doll.

Quietly I climbed down from the sleeping loft into the main room of the house. Mother and Will were arguing. I hid behind the grain barrels so that I could hear. In the glow of the firelight they leaned toward each other, their elbows on the table. My older sisters Annie and Mary looked on anxiously from their sewing and spinning.

"I've heard a family was killed only twenty miles away, near Manhattan Island," Will said.

For a moment I forgot to breathe. I hadn't known that the Indians around us had ever killed anyone.

Mother's thin mouth twitched. She looked sharp and pointed, like her white linen collar. "We've only just settled here, and we've had such a peaceful summer. The Indians are friendly. They brought us the fish."

"These two may be friends, but the rumors distress me," Will said.

"Will! What are we going to do?" my sister Annie asked.

"We must move away before the first snow."

"I'll have naught to do with it," Mother answered.

I took a trembling breath. *Oh, Mother,* I thought, *please listen to Will. Let us go to a place where there are streets and houses and lots of children. Let us move back to our old home, in Narragansett.*

Mother said, "I refuse to move this family again."

"Then Annie and I may have to leave you here," Will replied. "Annie is with child. I would not have us begin our family in a place that is not safe."

Annie and Will couldn't leave us! My five oldest brothers and sisters lived far away. If more of the family separated, I would not be able to stand it.

"Mother Hutchinson, you are a stubborn woman," Will said.

I cried out silently, *Mother! Listen to Will!* It had been Mother's idea to move to this wilderness. If it had not been for her, we would still be living in a town with our relatives and other neighbors.

Mother rose and took up a poker. She jabbed at one of the logs. Her white skin seemed translucent, her fingers bony and thin. "God gave me a vision. I saw an Indian girl and an English girl together, as friends. I *saw* them in my vision."

"A vision!" Will said. "Is a vision more important than our family's safety?"

"Mother, none of us likes it here," Annie said.

Mary nervously pumped the pedal of the spinning wheel. "Mother, please listen to us." I watched the big wheel go around.

"The Dutch call this place Vriedelandt, 'the land of peace,' " Mother went on. "It's another sign we should stay. This is our Promised Land. We will make the Indians our friends and show them God's mercy as God has shown us His mercy." Her eyes began to shine.

"We've planted ourselves down in the midst of trouble once again," said Will.

Trouble. That was the word people used the most when they talked to Mother or about her.

I stepped forward. "Can we move back to our old house?"

"We're going to stay here, Susanna. Why aren't you in bed?" Mother asked.

"Bad dreams."

Mother put her hands on my shoulders. "Everything is going to be all right. It's late now and you should go to sleep."

"I want to hear what you're saying!"

"What impertinence! Susanna, you are not yet ten years old. You cannot speak up like an adult!" Then Mother laughed. "You're exactly like me."

Mother turned me around and gave me a tender pat on my head. I felt the warmth of her fingers through my cap. "Annie, help put Susanna to bed."

Up in the loft, Annie tucked me in beside four of my sisters and brothers. "Why won't Mother listen to Will?" I whispered.

"Susanna, you know how Mother argues with people. Oh, how I wish Father were alive. He would know what to do!"

I missed Father so. He had died a year earlier, back in our old home. Father had been the only person who could talk reason to Mother. He understood her temperament and loved her even the more for it. For her he had moved halfway across the world, from England to Boston, because she said that God had spoken to her.

Mother had fire coursing through her veins, Father used to say. It was a fire that could warm a household, draw us all together, and make us comfortable and happy. But it was also a fire that could flare up and spread wildly, as in Boston when Mother had preached to large crowds, criticizing the ministers in the churches. No woman in the colonies had ever dared to speak in public. A leper, a witch, the authorities called her. Jezebel. They brought Mother to trial for disrupting the peace and for speaking falsehoods—heresy. They imprisoned her, then banished her from the Massachusetts Bay Colony. My mother, Anne Hutchinson, was the most notorious woman in all the colonies.

So Father moved our family again, from Boston to a wilderness territory called Narragansett. Others came with us, and the new settlement grew. After a few years soldiers from Boston threatened to take over our towns. Then Father died of a weak heart and we moved a third time, to this wilderness here. It was Dutch territory—where the authorities from Boston had no power over Mother.

In the dim light I looked at Annie. "Are you going to leave us?"

"No, Susanna. It would be too big a job for Mother to take care of all of you children without Will and me helping out."

I whispered, "Annie, if you and Will leave, then I'm

6

going with you! I don't care about Mother and the others!"

"Susanna, for shame! How could you even think of it? If one of us goes, we all go. Or else we all stay here."

"But what's going to happen to us?" I asked.

"Don't worry. Mother will learn to make peace with people, and they'll learn to make peace with her, too. We'll go back to Narragansett someday, or Boston. We won't have to run away anymore. I'll raise my child in a community with relatives and friends."

A town! To live in houses, side by side! "Mother doesn't want to go back," I said.

"If she thinks it's her idea, she'll go."

"But what if she doesn't change her mind? Then may I leave with you and Will?"

"Susanna! You're so stubborn. You are just like Mother!"

The Massacre

THE NEXT MORNING KATE AND I WALKED across the sloping meadow, a bucket in each hand.

The sky was blue above the yellow fields and tall trees. The cool waters of a creek came out of a shadowy growth of overhanging thicket, then flowed into the river. Shrubs grew down to the water's edge. A gentle wind touched my face.

It was warm for September, but I shivered when I thought of the previous day's visit. Why did the Indians come? What did they want from us?

"Over there, on the other side of the woods," I asked, "is that where the Indians grow their corn?"

"I think so," Kate answered.

"And where their village is?"

"Perhaps. Let's fill the water buckets now," she said. Kate bossed me because she was thirteen.

"Do you suppose we'll ever have a school here, Kate?"

"Not this year. Mother will probably give us our lessons again. There aren't enough families here for a school."

"I miss our big sisters," I said. "I wish I could tell Faith and Bridget about the Indians."

"I know. I wish we could all be together."

We filled our buckets, and I thought of my oldest brothers and sisters. Edward and Faith were in Boston with their own families, Bridget and Samuel were in Narragansett, and Richard was in faraway England.

I was surprised that I missed school and services so. In our former school the master had once whipped Kate for bringing in her doll. The clergy of our Puritan meeting house were even more strict. On Sundays all the family attended service for a few hours and had to sit very still. Then, after a midday meal, we returned to the meetinghouse for a few more hours. On the Lord's Day laughing was against the law.

Still, at least there were *people.* I could run from house to house, all lined up on either side of the street. We had lots of visitors. For dinner we had pork or perhaps roasted goose with apples. The adults discussed the sermon and questioned the children to see how much of the morning's lecture we remembered and understood.

For our new home Mother had chosen land near Long Island Sound, five miles from our neighbors, the Throckmortons and the Cornells. Will and my brothers had cut trees for the new house. Then we had all helped fill in the framework with clay, sand, and straw. We had moved rocks so that we could plant the fields. It was hard, lonely work.

"Mother doesn't seem afraid of the Indians," I said.

"We never had any trouble with the Narragansett Indians," Kate said.

"But they didn't paint their faces as they do here."

"Yes, they did. It's just that we were more familiar with them."

Kate was right. We had purchased land from the Narragansett Indians through our friend Roger Williams, who knew their language. Once, during a difficult winter, they had brought provisions to our family. But this time we had not been introduced to the Indians. Mother had bought our land from our English neighbor, John Throckmorton, who had purchased it from the Dutch.

The meadow spread out around us as we walked back to our tidy house, its chimney outlined against the sky. The smoky breeze carried the smell of roasting meat. Ahead of us our cow grazed, and in the distance Will chopped wood with my brothers Francis and William, while Mary and Mother soaked reeds to make baskets.

I stopped. "Kate!" Something was moving in the long grasses.

• • •

Twenty or thirty Indians rushed at the house, whooping and shouting and waving knives and flaming torches. Their bodies were painted red and blue and black.

I raced across the yard, screaming, "Mother! Mother!"

Indians ran into our home. One of them carried out a kettle. Another came out with Mother's red blankets. They must have slashed the beds—feathers flew everywhere. Fire crackled.

Tied to the fence, the dogs went into a frenzy, barking and struggling to be let go.

One Indian lunged at Will with a club and knocked him down.

Zuriel cowered near the house, screaming. I ran toward him as fire spread across the enclosure and the animals cried out.

The two Indians who had come the day before pulled Mother out of the house. The man with the snake on his forehead hit her with a stone axe, crushing her forehead. She fell down, dead.

"Mother!" I stood frozen.

"Run!" Kate gave me a push. I dashed away from the house. An Indian grabbed Kate and dragged her by her hair. He cut her neck, and blood gushed out as she crumpled to the ground.

I raced across the enclosure, crying. Mary ran toward the brook, chased by an Indian with a torch.

In the confusion of smoke and fire and terrifying faces, I thought I saw a figure in the distance waving to me.

"Susanna!" someone called.

I ran as fast as I could toward the voice, tripping over rocks. My face was wet, my heart was bursting.

An Indian leaped on me, and I fell backward. Three others grabbed me and twisted my arms. I shrieked. The tall snake-faced man ran toward me.

I looked up as he lifted his stone axe. Then he grinned, showing his cracked lips and terrible teeth. The snake on his forehead wrinkled. He spoke to the men who held me and they loosened their grip.

I kicked and hit the Indians on either side of me. "Let me go, let me go, let me go!"

They dragged me back to the house. The barn and the roof of the house burned wildly, the fire roaring. I was forced to walk among the bodies on the ground. Mother . . . Zuriel . . . Will . . . dead. I shut my eyes, screaming.

As the Indians carried me off into the tall grass, I looked back to see my house disappear in a black cloud of smoke.

• • •

The warrior with the bone nose ornament tied my hands behind my back and led me to the stream. I fell to my knees as the Indians washed themselves. Their clothes were soaked in blood.

We crossed the meadow, pushing through the brush as the trail wound into the marsh.

I felt dizzy. I trembled all over, feeling icy and cold. I wept. What were they going to do with me? Where were we going?

We walked single file on the narrow path, shaggy reeds on either side.

The Indian in front of me turned and said, *"Cheet-kwu-see!"*

I could not stop sobbing.

"Cheet-kwu-see!"

My feet sank down into the mud as I walked. I fell silent, biting my lips. Something rattled in the sack the man was carrying: my family's cooking pots. All through me, names pounded, over and over: Mother, Kate, Annie . . .

We reached another trail, where some of the party separated. The snake-faced man led me on.

The swamp opened up into a river. The Indians

dragged out two large canoes from the brush, and the snake-faced warrior took me and another Indian in his canoe. I sat on the damp floor of the boat with my family's goods wedged between my legs. We pushed off, and then I felt the canoe rise. We drifted out into the cool evening.

My family can't be dead, I thought. *No. Never.*

We moved quickly in the dim light, winding amidst the reeds, down, around, and bobbing up again. At times one of the Indians had to get out to push our canoe through the mud. As the sun set, a full moon rose.

I thought I heard voices, but they were in my mind. I remembered running through the field. Then I pictured my mother in her long black dress and pointed collar, standing in front of the hearth, saying, "God gave me a vision."

Mother should have listened to Will and Annie. I could have made her listen. It had been wrong of me to say what I did to Annie. . . . How could I have been angry with Mother?

Annie and Mary! They might also be alive. Perhaps they had escaped into the brush.

Someone had called to me, someone had tried to rescue me. Who was it? Thomas Cornell, our neighbor?

Mother, I called out silently. *Come and rescue me. Mother!*

I was startled from my thoughts as our canoe passed through two thick clouds of buzzing, biting mosquitoes. They flew into my face, but I hardly cared. The air was heavy with a pungent swamp scent. We traveled by moonlight. I looked at the snake-faced man and shivered. His eyes were clear and shining.

I felt I was in a dream. Somewhere animals were moving around us, and one dropped into the water from a nearby log. In the moonlight, hundreds of white birds dotted a grassy shore.

Those bodies. They couldn't have been my mother and my sisters and brothers.

The stream twisted through the swamp, then opened up to the sound. We were now surrounded by deep water, and directly in front of us rose the humped silhouette of a large island. If the boat overturned, I would drown. I did not know how to swim, but it didn't matter. I wanted to die.

The canoe landed on the rocky beach of the island. I put one foot into the cold water, then the other. They led me along a trail through the woods.

"My mother is dead!" I cried out, but I did not believe it. Yet these men with their painted faces and their stinking hides were real. Murderers were taking me somewhere.

All at once I mustered my courage. I dashed toward the dark trees, but the Indian with the bone in his nose caught me and hit me across the face.

I allowed him to lead me back to the others. I would wait. I would find a new opportunity.

The Village

FINALLY WE ARRIVED AT THE INDIAN VILLAGE. It was surrounded by a tall palisade of sticks. Inside was a circle of bark and mud huts. Some were long, others smaller and shaped like beehives. As we approached, women and children hurried out of these houses. Skinny dogs raced about.

"*Hoo!*" cried the warriors.

"*Hoo! Ka-yah!*" the villagers shouted back.

The tall, snake-faced warrior led the way. I followed close behind, on display. We marched around the village. Other men and boys joined in, whooping.

The procession stopped in the middle of the village, where a heavyset woman with long white hair stirred a broth over an open fire.

I heard someone shriek; it was my own voice. I began to cry.

The snake-faced man uttered something to the old woman. He nodded to her and took a step back, as if to say he had done his part and was now no longer responsible for me. The old woman grunted.

I wailed, "Mother! Mother!"

The woman talked back to the warrior sternly, and

he frowned. Then she looked at me sympathetically. But she was horrid. She had more wrinkles than I'd ever seen, and she had a big red circle painted on each cheek. All the women and girls painted themselves this way. The girls did not even cover their heads with caps; they wore their hair loose and tangled.

I cried and shrieked until the wrinkled woman put a hand on my shoulder. Would she hit me? Kill me? *Whatever is happening will soon be over,* I thought.

She looked me in the eye and pointed to herself. "Som-kway."

"Wam-pak," the snake-faced man said.

"You killed my mother!" I screamed at him. "I hate you! I hate all of you!"

"Cheet-kwu-see!" the woman said softly. She drew me toward her, but I shrank back, breathing in her fishy odor. I wept, and this time she did not try to comfort me.

A crowd moved toward us. A young woman stepped forward to get a close look at me. She was slender with a wide face and high cheekbones. Over her bare chest she wore many beaded necklaces. *"Say-hay!"* she said coldly. I could tell she was proud by the way she held herself. She looked much like the other women, except that she had a thinner mouth and a stiffer air. I knew she had taken an instant dislike to me. She was accompanied by a boy and a girl who looked at me curiously. The girl was about my own age and was naked to the waist. The boy was a few years younger.

"I'm not afraid of you!" I shouted.

The warriors presented my family's goods to the old woman. She took an interest in the woven blankets and a cooking pot. Then she led me to a nearby fire and gestured to me to sit near her. Others sat on the ground, far from the fire. The children hardly wore any clothing, despite the chill in the air. Many women had bare chests, with only a loose fur or shawl over their shoulders, and knee-length deerskin skirts. They jabbered in their strange language.

Meanwhile a group of boys added wood to the fire as the drumming began. Then I knew: *I'm going to be sacrificed. Lord help me, let it go quickly. Here it is.* I held my breath. *Now I will be killed—like my family.* I tried to hold my head high.

The men and boys began to dance in procession. A stocky older man went first, followed by Wam-pak. When I looked at him, I felt something cold brush my heart. They danced around to a fast, shrieking song with a rapid drumbeat, raising their knees and sometimes extending their arms above their heads. The song changed into a noisy, sorrowful wailing. After a while they seemed to repeat the fast shrieking.

The women clapped and cheered. More dances followed, all unreal and dreamlike. Time passed slowly as I listened to my own shallow breathing. Sometimes the boys bowed low, with their raggedy hair sweeping the ground. It seemed the dance would never end. I suddenly vomited. "God, please help me!" I prayed aloud. "God, lead me away from here. I want my mother! I want my mother!"

I let the tears flow. After a while the very wrinkled old woman, Som-kway, led me away to one of the huts. The mother and her two children followed us.

The house seemed like a cave, and it smelled moldy and rank. There was one long, dark room lit by firelight. Dried plants and corncobs hung from the ceiling, and platforms ran along the sides. Two small fires burned near the center of the room, heating clay food pots in their ashes. Smoke from the fire curled up through an open hole in the ceiling. A mangy dog with pointed ears sat on the rushes covering the floor and looked up as we entered.

"Mu-sha-kay!" the old woman, Som-kway, said, and indicated that I should sit on the floor with the others.

She scooped some cornmeal mush out of the pot for me into a wooden bowl. My head was spinning. I did not touch the food, so after a while she put the mush back into the clay pot. She handed me water in a gourd, and I drank a little. The mother scowled at me in the dim light. The children stared.

Som-kway pointed to each of them in turn. She called the woman Suk-ee-loon-gawn, the little boy Mee-kwun, and the girl Sa-kat.

By now I was almost sure that the women did not plan to kill me. But just then a tall figure pushed his way past the hide that served as a door. Wam-pak.

He spoke to them and gave me a passing glance, a half smile. Then he left to join the drumming and singing outside. A chill ran through me. This house was his house. The woman was his wife, the older woman his mother or mother-in-law perhaps, and the children were his. Was I to be their slave?

After a while the children were put to bed on the platforms. The women argued loudly. It seemed that Som-kway wanted me to sleep next to the other children, toward the front of the house, but Suk-ee-loon-gawn refused. In the end I was led to sleep on the part of the platform near the back, in a storage area.

As I lay on the hard bed of sticks, I stared at the shadows of corncobs hanging from the ceiling. Why hadn't the Indians killed me?

I missed the feel of my pillows and featherbed, my rag dolls, and my sleeping brothers and sisters. Too frightened to close my eyes, I listened. After some time Som-kway began to snore. The little boy cried out once and was silenced by his mother. Outside the drums beat slowly.

The image of the bodies on the ground came to me. How many of my brothers and sisters had survived the attack? When would they rescue me?

I remembered the only other time I had been separated from my mother, when I was about four years old. We'd been living in Boston in a grand house, which had a great fireplace that opened to the sky. The governor had arrested my mother and held her prisoner for four months. It was spring when Mother returned. A dazzling late snow hung on all the trees. I waded through the snow to greet Mother as she struggled toward me, fell, then picked herself up again. I was shocked; her face was drawn and pale and she was too thin, aside from her pregnant belly.

"Mother!" I called out. "Mother!" As she embraced me I let the tears roll down my cheeks. She was not her spry, feisty self at all.

I heard my mother's high voice. "We need to go someplace where we are *safe*," she said. Each time she had said those words, the family broke apart. In Boston I had been one of twelve children; in Narragansett, one of ten. In the Dutch territory I had been one of seven. Now . . .

Now I was alone.

God help me! I prayed silently. I tried to remember the psalm my mother had taught me to say before I went to sleep each night: *The Lord is my shepherd; I shall not want. . . .*

The fire died down and the long house was almost completely dark. Some time later the ceremonies outside ended. Wam-pak entered the house, and I listened to my heart beat as he groped his way about. He brushed past me. Then he lay down on a sleeping platform, so close that I could hear him breathe.

For many hours I lay there, terrified, wrapped in my family's red woolen blankets.

The Deer

THE NEXT MORNING I OPENED MY EYES TO find the Indian girl staring at me. I thought I was dreaming. Then came the shock.

My mother would not be calling me to come for my porridge. I would not be milking the cow or carrying in water from the stream.

I wanted to scream, but I had screamed and cried the day before, and that had only made the Indians angry. From this day I determined I would not show any sign of weakness. Mother would be proud of me if I was strong.

The girl kept staring at me. She smelled of smoke and musky, damp hides. She and I were alone in the long house. In the night the house had been cavernous and cluttered with hanging corncobs. But now sunlight broke in through an open doorway to the bright-spotted green and yellow woods outside. *How can this place be beautiful when my mother is dead?* I thought. *Mother, please come. Take me home.*

As I sat up the girl grinned at me. She had a space between her square front teeth and had pink circles painted over her wide cheeks. She did not look very clean. Her chest was bare, but she did not seem ashamed. She was thinner than I and had wide-set eyes. She wore her long black hair gathered in back with a greasy string.

"Sa-kat," she said, pointing to herself cheerfully.

She pointed to me. I was silent.

I crawled out from under the blankets and sat up on the platform.

Sa-kat added some more wood to the fire to warm the corn mush, which was still in the clay pot from the night before. She scooped the thick yellow mush into a wooden bowl and offered it to me along with a clam-shell.

I watched Sa-kat serve herself. I was very hungry, so I took a bite. The mush was mixed with maple syrup. To my surprise it tasted like one of my mother's puddings.

After I ate, I stood and put on my shoes. I peeked out of the flap over the back doorway. Was Wam-pak lurking about?

The woods sloped in back of the long house. Where was the privy? I crept into the woods a few paces and did what I had to do behind a tree.

Sa-kat kept me within her sight. Perhaps the older ones had instructed her to guard me. I thought about running away, but I was on an island and I probably couldn't go very far. So I let Sa-kat lead me up the hill, around the front of the long house, and into the clearing.

My heart thumped at the sight of so many Indians. The clearing bustled with activity. Women and girls—supervised by the old woman, Som-kway—split and gutted fish, then hung them on twiggy lattices to dry.

Some boys were burning out the inside of a log and scraping it with tools. Haughty Suk-ee-loon-gawn was grinding meal in a hollowed-out tree stump. She moved close and looked me in the eye. *"Shu-wa-nuk-kooh-kway,"* she said with scorn; then she spit. I jumped back. The spit ran down my cheek and I wiped it away. We glared at each other.

Some of the girls crowded around me. They reached out and picked up my long red hair. "Leave me alone!" I shouted, startling them. Then I pushed them away.

Wam-pak and another man emerged from the woods, dragging a huge antlered buck on a kind of wooden frame. They deposited it at Som-kway's feet.

"Eh-chay!" Som-kway hooted, and made some shrill animal sounds. She was obviously delighted.

I froze. What would Wam-pak do to me?

Wam-pak and the old woman dragged the deer and placed it across a log with its head up. Its six-pointed antlers were fuzzy and soft.

Wam-pak left the clearing. The old woman called to Sa-kat and told her to fetch something. She returned with a deerskin bag, from which the old woman took out some small stone knives. She handed one to Sa-kat and one to me. I jerked back. Som-kway expected me to help her butcher the deer!

Som-kway made the first cut along the center of the buck's white belly. She was showing me what she wanted me to do.

At that moment I learned it was not necessary for two people to speak the same language in order to have an argument. I looked right into Som-kway's dark eyes. "No!" I said.

She eyed me.

"I refuse!" I said.

"Cheet-kwu-see!" Her tone was fierce.

Sa-kat looked on sympathetically.

Reluctantly I reached for the buck's soft fur. I picked up the stone-bladed knife, but I could not make the cut.

Som-kway grabbed my hands. She took two fingers of my left hand and inserted them into the cut she had made. Then she guided my right hand so that I carved a straight line all the way to the animal's tail with the stone knife. The hide pulled away from the incision. Soon my hands were covered with blood and buzzing flies. A vapor rose from the still-warm meat.

I rushed to the edge of the clearing and vomited.

It was Sa-kat's turn to help; I turned away so that I wouldn't see what she was doing. My hands and my dress were bloody. I scowled at the women who were looking on. Why weren't *they* butchering the deer? My mother and older sisters had butchered pigs while I stayed in the house to watch my little brother. "What are you looking at?" I snapped.

The old woman forced me to make more cuts along the chest and abdomen. Between stages she showed me how to clean my knife with moss.

Quickly Som-kway reached into the body cavity, cut loose the inner organs, and put them in a clay pot.

I swatted away flies as the old woman tilted the carcass so that the blood ran out. Then she instructed Sa-kat and me to wipe the cavity using moss and leaves. This was the very worst part. The deer was left to hang in the breeze near the long house.

Som-kway nodded. She hooted and made a strange, guttural laughing sound. Tears ran down my face.

Next Sa-kat led me through the woods and down to a wide beach. What was happening? The girl gestured that we should wash ourselves in the cold, salty water.

As I cleaned the blood from my hands I stared at them, thinking of the blood that had been on Wampak's hands when he killed my mother.

I had not allowed myself to cry all morning, but now I broke into tears. My mother was dead, and probably most of my brothers and sisters as well. I was a captive, living among people who did bloody, savage things.

God, deliver me from this awful place, I prayed. *Mother. Mother. Someone, help.*

Sa-kat looked at me and a tear started at the corner of her eye. She was crying, too! Did she understand how I felt?

She tried to take my hand, but I pushed her away and stared straight ahead, listening to the waves crash on the shore. The wind felt strong and cold on my wet arms and face.

A dark, curved body broke the surface of the water and jumped high in the air. A porpoise. No, it was a whole school of porpoises. My father and I had spent hours watching them in Narragansett.

Sa-kat shrieked with joy. She pointed, babbling. Finally I met her eyes. She smiled at me, but I turned away.

We watched the water together for quite a while, then returned to the hut, where Som-kway clothed me in a deerskin skirt and a raggedy raccoon shawl. The old woman took my bloody dress away. I followed her out of the hut, thinking she was going to wash it. To my horror, she threw it onto a fire.

"No!" I called out. "That was my new dress!" My sister Annie had made it for me. I tried to pull it out of the fire, but the dress was ruined.

I thought of the massacre, of the burning house, of the bodies on the ground, as I watched my new dress shrivel in the orange flames. It was the last thing I had had that was mine.

Adoption

DAYS TURNED TO WEEKS. EVERY MORNING I canoed over to the fields just west of the island with the women and girls. Sa-kat showed me how to paddle, but I didn't try very hard.

We harvested the last of the ripened corn. It was strenuous, hard labor for only the female members of the village. My skin was grimy and my hair dirty and tangled.

My hands automatically did the work, but my thoughts and hopes were of rescue. Surely it had been Thomas Cornell who had called my name on the day of the massacre. It was only a matter of time until he came to bring me back to his family. Perhaps some of my brothers and sisters had escaped the attack. I even imagined my mother was somehow alive and waiting to welcome me. Each night I collected a pebble to mark the number of days I had spent with the Indians. My secret pile grew: two weeks, three weeks, one month. When would they come for me?

The Indians grew their corn on small mounds, planted together in tangled masses with squash, pumpkins, and beans. These hills were arranged in ten rows, making up several hundred hills. We broke off the ears of corn and afterward stuffed them into woven bags. All the while Sa-kat chattered to me in the Indians' shrill tongue, repeating certain words again and again. I still thought this girl extremely dirty and wild, but I listened enough to learn a little of her language.

"I am Susanna," I told Sa-kat. She seemed so delighted that I taught her a few more English words: *sky, tree, fur,* and *beads.*

Sa-kat pointed to an enormous clear paw print in the mud near the cornfield. *"Mah-kwa,"* she said.

I guessed it was a bear print.

This added to my fears. I was always on the alert for danger. It took me a long time to fall asleep, when I slept at all. I startled quickly if there was a noise. Usually I was conscious enough to be afraid when Wampak entered the long house. Would he grab me? All day and all night I was frightened in a way I had never known before.

If I was not rescued soon, I would run away. But if I ran away, I'd need to know the lay of the land. Between me and whatever family I had left was a vast wilderness full of wolves, bears, and other fearsome creatures.

• • •

A flock of wild turkeys fed in the afternoons in the weedy patches between the corn hills. Once a pack of boys, holding their bows high, rushed into the field and scattered the flock. They yelped like turkeys, drew, and released their arrows. The turkeys galloped and took to the air. One flew right toward my face, beating its wings furiously. I was so surprised, I dropped my bundle of corn and beans.

Suk-ee-loon-gawn ordered the boys out of the fields. I imagined she was saying, "Get out of my fields! You're destroying the corn hills, you rascals."

The boys slunk away. Sa-kat and the other girls giggled. For the first time in weeks I had a moment where I was almost enjoying myself.

Gradually the woods turned the color of flame and the air became rich with the smell of autumn leaves. The Indian girls and I gathered baskets of chestnuts. My arms grew sore from pounding the nuts and dried corn into meal. The men and boys trapped fish in a fencelike enclosure, and then there were the gutting and the drying to do.

Wam-pak was often gone for days at a time now, hunting or perhaps fighting. I grew accustomed to his stern face. His wife, Suk-ee-loon-gawn, was growing increasingly heavy, as my sister Annie had been. Was she pregnant? She was far less concerned with me than she had been in the beginning.

One day the men returned with twelve deer, partially butchered. We finished preparing the meat but did not eat it. The whole village, about a hundred people, suddenly moved to some large, empty huts on the other side of the island. What was going to happen? The fear rose up in me.

For the next week we did not have to work. Food was offered in abundance and I ate roasted venison, dipped in grease and maple sugar, until my stomach hurt. Like the Indians, I held it in my hands and hungrily lifted it to my dripping mouth. I remembered the feasts that my family had on the Lord's Day, with all of us children standing at the table, eating silently, carefully using our spoons and knives.

Now I didn't care if I had lost all my good English table manners.

In the evenings the villagers crowded into an enormous square house. I was not allowed to enter. Someone always stayed to guard me, while the deep, ghostly chants spiraled out into the cool night air.

On one feast day I stood on the beach alone watching the gulls drop clams onto the rocks. Som-kway and Sa-kat talked nearby. Suddenly they grabbed me, then removed my skirt and fur shawl. I stood naked, feeling ashamed and afraid. "Give me my clothes!" I screamed. Then the old woman hurled me into the icy water.

I fought, but her grip was surprisingly strong. I kicked and tried to drag her into the water with me. "I'm going to kill you first!" I said. I bit her hand, but she kept a firm grasp on me. She scrubbed me all over with a clump of slimy brown seaweed. She dunked me once, then pulled me out of the water again. As I stood on the beach shivering, she wrapped me in her own huge bear-fur cloak.

"You pretended to be my friend," I said to Sa-kat in English. "I was right not to trust you!" She lowered her eyes.

Next Som-kway and Sa-kat dragged me to a small hut of mud and bark that had a hot fire burning inside. Were they going to cook me and eat me? Unlike the other Indian houses, this hut did not have a hole on top for smoke to escape. It was a giant oven! Som-kway poured water over the hot stones in the fire, which sizzled and filled the hut with steam. Then she forced me, naked, into the hut and shut me inside. I cried and screamed, beating my fists on the walls. I could not find a way out. The hot steam surrounded me and filled my mouth with a bitter, charred taste. I began to sweat. Soon I felt too weak and dizzy to struggle. I prepared myself to die. In an odd way I looked forward to it. *God, help me!* I prayed. *Please let this be over quickly.*

But Som-kway opened the door of the hut. *"Peel-seet!"* she said, pleased. I staggered out, faint. I was alive after all! My skin was bright red. Som-kway laughed, showing her yellow teeth. Then once again Som-kway and Sa-kat dragged me down to the shore and dunked me in the freezing-cold water. When I stepped out, Som-kway warmed me in her thick cloak. I felt shaken but invigorated, clean, as if my mother had just bathed me beside our hearth. The cool wind blew on my wet hair.

Inside another hut, Som-kway and Sa-kat greased my body, then dressed me in a new raccoon shawl and deerskin skirt. Som-kway put soft deerskin moccasins on my feet and hung beaded shell necklaces around my neck. Sa-kat painted red circles on my cheeks. She gently combed my hair and tied it back with sinew. As miserable and confused as I was, I enjoyed this attention. I was reminded of times I had spent alone with my sisters; it had been so long since I had felt any sort of belonging.

How strange these people were, thinking up terrible tortures for me one minute and treating me kindly the next. More ceremonies followed that day. Som-kway led me into the smoky ceremonial house, where the villagers gathered around me. The old woman called Wam-pak, Suk-ee-loon-gawn, Sa-kat, and young Mee-kwun to stand near me. Sa-kat grinned and squeezed my hand. Chanting, Som-kway took a pinch of tobacco from a small deerskin pouch and tossed it on the fire. While moaning, groaning, and chanting some more, she filled a short stone pipe with tobacco, which she lit from the fire. She puffed on it a few times.

Som-kway seemed to look right through me as she chanted. I heard her say, *"Nin-gu-mee-pah-kee-now"* several times, then simply *"Mee-pahk."* I understood Mee-pahk to be my new name.

"No!" I said, shaking my head. "My name is Susanna! You must call me Susanna."

"Mee-pahk," Som-kway replied firmly.

"No! Susanna!" Som-kway and I faced each other. Something precious was being taken from me, but I had no choice. I had to obey.

Next Som-kway offered me water from a gourd dipper and bowl. She tilted the dipper and I drank from it. Everyone drank in turn. The old woman gave me a gift, my own small deerskin pouch, which held a pretty crystal rock, feathers, and a few smooth stones, which I guessed had some magical significance.

A large meal of venison followed. There was much talking and chatter the rest of the afternoon, though I could understand only a few words, such as *meet-see,* "eat." That night, inside the big ceremonial house, the boys and men drummed and danced. As the men circled around and around, all dissolved into a single frightening painted face—Wam-pak's.

The Fur Traders

SA-KAT TAUGHT ME MANY INDIAN WORDS IN
the next weeks. She was eager for me to learn her language so that she could talk to me. I had been brooding
in silence for months, and now, I decided, I would ven-
ture to say some of the Indian words out loud. Before
long I understood and could pronounce many of the
Indians' names or nicknames—they went by one or the
other or both. Long names were shortened for everyday
conversation.

Som-kway meant Great Woman and Wam-pak
meant White Tree. Wam-pak's wife, Suk-ee-loon-gawn,
was Black Wing Woman. I thought Sa-kat's name,
Emerging Flower Woman, suited her well. Sa-kat's little
brother, Mee-kwun, had a nickname that meant
Feather. My own name, Mee-pahk, meant Pretty Leaf.
A leaf is a pretty thing, Sa-kat explained: A leaf can turn
bright colors, a leaf can change.

I also learned that the Indians I was living with were
Algonquians called Lenape, meaning "the people," and
that this band were also called Siwanoy or Sha-wa-no-
wuk, "the people of the south." The land around us,
including the islands, they called Lenape-haw-king; and

our village and our island were both referred to as Lap-ha-wah-king, Place of Stringing Beads.

The afternoons turned dark and cold. By the number of daily pebbles I had gathered in my secret pile near the long house I guessed about three months had passed. It was late November, so I was now ten years old.

Oh, how I missed Mother! I had been angry with her because she couldn't seem to get along with people. Now I thought, *Mother, forgive me. I love you. Mother, take me away from here.*

It was about this time that the fur traders came to our village. It was early in the afternoon, some hours before darkness. The older Indian boys had brought in dozens of fat squirrels. The girls and I were skinning them when, though an opening in the trees, we noticed a sailing ship. White men! We tore our way through the brush and ran down to the beach. I shrieked as I ran. I was going to be saved. At last!

Soon the whole village stood on the shore. The vessel was a Dutch sloop, with one tall mast and its mainsail flapping in the wind. A rowboat was lowered, and three men came ashore. My heart beat wildly as I stood among the crowd of Indian girls.

A husky, red-faced man wearing a jacket with slashed sleeves was the first to land. He was followed by a man about six feet tall, who stooped slightly. Both carried muskets. The third was a boy of about fourteen or fifteen. All three wore rich collars of lace, white stockings, and hats with plumes. They were Dutch; the English never dressed so lavishly.

My eyes feasted on familiar things. Shoes. Hats. Pale skin. A ship with sails. I wanted to scream with excitement. But I had to wait until the right moment to talk to them.

"*He!*" the husky Dutchman greeted Wam-pak.

"*He!*" Wam-pak said in return.

Wam-pak invited the men to the village to feast on squirrel meat and corn, but the visitors refused. The Dutchman took out blue glass beads from a bag he was carrying. Wam-pak seemed mesmerized by them. As he fingered the beads a group of young warriors stood around him, holding their long, curved bows and quivers of arrows. Mah-kwa, or Bear, Som-kway's much younger brother, eyed the white men nervously. He was the holy man of the tribe.

My heart pounded. I waited for the Dutchmen to notice me. I was sure they would know that I was not one of the Lenape.

"Beads," Wam-pak said in English. My head jerked up when I heard him. He must have picked up the word from Sa-kat, who had learned it from me.

The men began to trade, speaking Lenape. For the blue beads, a bit of red cloth, fishhooks, a sewing needle, an iron axe and hoe, and a thick green bottle of rum, Wam-pak traded dried corn, fish, pumpkin rings, a raccoon pelt, beaver skins, and a worn beaver-skin jacket. The Indian men immediately started to drink the rum, passing the bottle one to another, as Som-kway frowned and crossed her arms. The only man not to drink was her brother, Mah-kwa.

"You have no more skins?" the Dutchman asked.

"This is all," Wam-pak answered.

Som-kway tried to hold me back, but I pushed my way through the crowd. "I'm a captive!" I said. "Help me!"

The trader with the slashed sleeves took in the situation at a glance, and my heart leaped. First he spoke to me in Dutch. Then in English.

"You're an English girl, captured. Is that right?"

"Yes."

"I'd heard there were English hereabouts. What is your name?"

"Susanna Hutchinson."

Wam-pak frowned as I related the story of the massacre to the visitors. "Are the Cornells and the Throckmortons still alive?" I asked.

"I have never heard of those names," the Dutchman replied. He went on to say he'd thought the colony of New Netherland had made peace with the Indians, though he said he wasn't surprised there had again been trouble. He told me that Governor Kieft at Fort Amsterdam was a poor leader who made trouble with the Indians even though the Dutch colonists were greatly outnumbered. In all of New Netherland there were only about two hundred fifty Dutch settlers and about fifty or sixty soldiers. As for the "heathen," he thought they numbered a few thousand.

The Dutchmen talked among themselves while the Indians looked on expectantly.

"Please, won't you take me with you?" I begged. There was so much feeling in my voice that the Dutch boy said something to the others.

"We will take you to the fort," the captain agreed. "It is less than a day's journey from here." He signaled to the boy to drag the boat from the beach to the water. I stepped toward the boat, my blood racing. How quickly good fortune had come to me! Sa-kat looked miserable.

"Leave her here. She is ours," Wam-pak called out.

Suk-ah-sun, or Black Rock, stepped toward the Dutchmen with his spear raised. He was the bone-nosed warrior who had helped Wam-pak to kill my mother.

The tallest of the three Dutchmen leveled his musket. There was a thundering sound. I screamed and threw my hands over my face. Suk-ah-sun fell dead.

The husky Dutchman smacked the killer across the face. He ordered the others to get back into the boat as the Indians drew their arrows.

An arrow pierced the Dutch boy in the shoulder. I ran after the Dutchmen as they scurried to their boat. As they pulled away from shore the captain called, "We'll come back for you!"

I ran into the water after the boat. "Wait!" I was almost in reach of them. Wam-pak pulled me back. I wrestled with him. "Let me go!"

Wam-pak looked at me angrily, his eyes dark and clear.

I stood shaking, hardly hearing him. "Mee-pahk, you are our daughter now," he said in Lenape.

"I'm not your daughter."

"Mee-pahk, you are my daughter and I am your father. I will protect you as a father."

Suk-ah-sun lay dead on the beach. His wife began to beat her chest with her fists.

I looked at Suk-ah-sun's body and felt sick. I had been responsible for a man's death. I cried out to the Dutchmen, who were now too far away to hear, "Don't leave me! Don't leave me here!"

I turned to Wam-pak. *I hate you,* I said silently. *I wish you were dead, too.* Both men had killed my family. They deserved to die.

I stood on the beach with Wam-pak, staring out at the deep, blue water, which was choppy from the driving wind. I watched the sails of the Dutch sloop flap as the vessel pulled away. At that moment I began to give up hope of ever being rescued.

A Burial

As the villagers prepared Suk-ah-sun's body I stood nearby in shock. They smeared red paint on his face. Then they murmured a song, low and dark and mournful. I was surprised that they didn't seem angry with me or blame me for the death. The villagers just ignored me, as if I did not exist. I felt no remorse for Suk-ah-sun. I turned back to look at the water. How close I had come to freedom! Would the Dutch ship ever come back for me?

The mood of the villagers was somber, but the following night there was a feast. The day after that, Suk-ah-sun was buried in a graveyard on the mainland. His warrior friends rolled his body up into a crouching position, holding his curved bow and quiver of arrows, Sakat explained, so that he could use them in the hunting lands of the spirit world.

The women in Suk-ah-sun's family had cut their hair off and blackened their faces with soot. *Now you know what it is to lose someone dear to you,* I thought. But as Suk-ah-sun's widow cried and shrieked, her blackened face contorted, I began to cry. I looked at Suk-ah-sun's eyes, and for a second I thought I saw my father's eyes. I could not help thinking of that day over a year earlier in Narragansett, when my father had been discovered dead on the road.

"Will Hutchinson is dead!" a boy had called out as he ran into our house.

"No! No!" Mother cried, jumping up from the table.

A few hours later, friends brought Father's body back to us in a cart. I was afraid to look at him.

"Will, my dear Will!" Mother cried out as she ran toward the cart.

That awful morning was cold and sunny. The trees had turned magnificent colors of orange and gold. *Please, God, bring Father back to life,* I prayed.

The physician examined my father. "A weak heart," he said.

"He worried himself too much over the welfare of our settlement," Mother said.

In the month before Father died, he had seemed older to me, his face pale and his hair graying. Sometimes he was short of breath. After the family had fled from Boston, Mother had said we would all begin a new life, away from controversy and politics. She did not like it when Father was chosen as a magistrate of the settlement. But soon the fires in Mother rose again.

My parents argued with the people who wanted to govern Narragansett in the same strict, oppressive way the Massachusetts Bay Colony was run. They and our friend Roger Williams wanted church and state to be separate; they did not believe anyone should be forced to belong to a particular church. "Let the sisters and brethren worship as they please," Mother said.

Soon the Massachusetts Bay Colony threatened to take over our settlement. Bay Colony soldiers raided one of our little towns. Roger Williams left for England to ask the king for a charter so that our four towns could become a colony. Then we would all be safe. But Mother became tired of waiting for Roger Williams to return. She and Father decided to move to New Netherland.

But then my own dear father died, so we had to make the journey without him.

Mother prepared his body. She put him in a coffin in his clean linen shirt with a square-cut collar, breeches, his square-toed shoes. His arms lay against his sides, and his hands were folded together. Mother covered Father with a shroud. Seeing him there gave me such a dread and lonely feeling that I was not able to go too close to him. Zuriel, then five years old, asked me, "When is Father going to wake up?"

I repeated Mother's words: "He will not rise again until the Judgment Day."

My sister Kate and I talked of angels.

"Do you see them?" I asked.

"See what?" she said.

There were about thirty angels around our father that day. I saw their outlines, standing motionless, side by side behind the coffin.

"Shadowy figures," I said. "I think they're angels, but they don't have wings."

She gasped. "You're like Mother, a visionary."

"Don't tell her! Please don't tell anyone," I cried.

It was dangerous to have special gifts. When my family had sailed from England on the ship *Griffin* when I was a baby, Mother had astonished everyone by prophesying the exact time the ship would arrive at port, several weeks earlier than expected. Later the magistrates used this as proof of witchcraft. Then once, when my sister Faith was seventeen years old, Faith had a vision about a boy being rescued at sea. Mother told everyone about it and word got back to the magistrates. "Like a witch, she has endowed her own daughter with forbidden powers," they said.

I watched the angels for over an hour. They didn't move once. When darkness fell, they disappeared.

Why was I able to see presences that my sisters and brothers could not? All I wanted was to be like everyone else. Not like Mother. People called Mother trouble; I did not want to be trouble's daughter.

After the funeral our house was crowded with visitors. My parents had had a rare marriage, people said, because it had been a marriage of equals. Father had always supported her; he had never tried to hold her back. Mother wept and told stories about my father. She told of the time when, about two years before Father's death, four men from Boston had arrived. Their purpose was to try to convince the people of Narragansett to return to the fold. They said that Mother could return to the church of Boston if she ceased public speaking.

The four men had interviewed Father privately. They said, "Control your wife. She is stubborn and opinionated!"

He had said, "My wife is a dear saint and a servant of God."

"You are a man of weak parts!"

Father had ordered the men to leave the house.

I felt a painful throbbing in my forehead. I looked up. Where was I? I slowly brought myself back to the Indians.

The ceremony had ended. The warriors put the last bit of dirt over Suk-ah-sun's body and placed a plain wooden stick to mark the grave.

Som-kway took my arm. "Your mind is crowded and confused," she seemed to say. I was beginning to understand her. She took me to the long house and gave me a foul-tasting hot drink, which helped me to sleep.

In the morning I looked out at the water and imagined that I saw the Dutch ship in the distance. I imagined it taking me to my mother or to Kate, who were somewhere waiting for me. At night I slept restlessly. Perhaps I was feeling some remorse for Suk-ah-sun's death after all. The villagers eyed me suspiciously.

Som-kway sometimes showed concern for me, but she did not often talk to me. I knew my place around her. Suk-ee-loon-gawn either ignored me or insulted me, calling me *shu-wa-nuk-kooh-kway,* meaning "white person" or "salt person." Pregnant, Suk-ee-loon-gawn spent more time resting in the long house, sewing hides into clothing or stringing beads into necklaces. She ordered me about: "You! Salt person! Bring me my food!"

Sa-kat alone stayed by my side, but my longing for the Dutch ship stood between us.

A Birth

WAM-PAK WAS ABSENT FOR DAYS AT A TIME with the men, following the deer and leaving the younger boys of the village behind to trap the squirrels and raccoons. Whenever he was at home, Wam-pak tried to talk with me. I could understood many words now. "It is the way of our people to hunt when the air is cold, when the animals' fur is thick and their bodies fat, when they do not give birth to their young," he told me. "You are learning much, Mee-pahk. You are learning our language. I am pleased."

I nodded and looked down at my feet.

"Many of our people are angry about Suk-ah-sun. Still, they accept you because you are my daughter. They will not harm you."

But I did not feel safe around him. My protector! I never knew if the men went off to hunt game or to kill the white settlers.

I asked Sa-kat, "Is there a war still going on? Do the warriors go off to fight in the winter?"

"Mostly they hunt, but sometimes they fight. You will see," Sa-kat said.

"Does Wam-pak ever bring back other captives?"

"No," she replied. "You are the only one."

I looked at her and thought: *Does she know that her father killed children?* But all I said was, "Why? What does he want from me?"

"A daughter," she said.

• • •

For a long time I saw no signs of the war, though the girls and women of the village rolled up balls of grease and sunflower seeds for the men to take with them to battle. Then a few lone Indian survivors of a massacre joined our tribe. They were our neighbors the Wiechquaeskeck. The Dutch had burned several of their villages, along with their corn supply.

Snow fell on the wigwams and long houses, on our noses, on our fur wrappings. My growing pile of pebbles indicated that December had come and gone. The bare trees lashed back and forth in the wind. We ate the corn, beans, and sunflower seeds stored in the deep pits within our long house and stayed inside. Som-kway and Suk-ee-loon-gawn taught Sa-kat and me to sew hides with bone needles. That winter Som-kway's two nephews, nicknamed Chah-kol, Frog, and Tu-ma, Beaver Hand, came to our long house for Som-kway's storytelling. They were thin, leggy boys of about my age. The boys whittled and shaped pieces of wood while Sa-kat and I sewed or played with Mee-kwun. I could not always follow Som-kway's strange stories, but I grew to like the deep, lilting quality of her voice. As I heard the same stories over and over, I began to understand the language much better.

Suk-ee-loon-gawn gave birth late that winter. The women's hut was away from the village in a grove of tall, fragrant pines, carpeted by layers of pine needles. Like our village, this place had fresh springs for drinking water close by. The women lived there during their monthly cycles. Now Suk-ee-loon-gawn moved to the women's hut, accompanied by Som-kway. Sa-kat and I brought them corn mush, called *sa-pan,* and dried meat. She could eat food only from serving sticks, for if she touched it, people feared, the spirits hovering around would poison the food for everyone else.

The women of the village gathered on the night of the birth, just as the women had done when there was a birth in Narragansett. My mother had been a midwife, and unlike most children, I knew something about birthing. Still, I was struck by the wonder and the horror of it. I stood close to Sa-kat as Suk-ee-loon-gawn squatted on her bed of furs and skins, half naked and clutching a pole in pain, her broad stomach stretched out. Despite my dislike for her, I felt sorry for her.

Som-kway and Sa-kat talked to Suk-ee-loon-gawn, encouraging her. The contractions were intense and painful. The baby descended until its head was clearly visible. It was wet and wrinkled.

Suk-ee-loon-gawn bore down and pushed. The shoulders emerged; then the entire body slid out with a gush of blood. Som-kway tied the cord and cut it with a stone knife.

An odd feeling came over me. I remembered the day, back in Narragansett, when Mother gave birth for the sixteenth and last time, with my older sisters helping her. I had crept into the room after it was over.

Mother's baby was blue and lifeless. First one sister and then another hit him on the back. Everyone waited for his breath. But no amount of shaking would make him come alive.

"No!" Mother cried out when she realized her child was dead. Faith dried the baby and put him on Mother's lap. Mother trembled all over, as all of us were trembling. She picked him up and rocked him.

Though he was dead, he was perfectly formed.

Later the clergy in Boston said that Mother's baby had horns and scales and feet like a chicken's and that Mother had given birth to a devil. This was offered as proof, along with Mother's visions, that she was a witch. Mother's friend Mary Dyer had recently miscarried, and the Boston magistrates suspected her of witchcraft as well. They dug up Mary Dyer's dead baby girl to see if it too had horns, scales, and chicken feet. The magistrates spread the word that both women had delivered monsters.

Now Som-kway slapped Suk-ee-loon-gawn's new son, and he gurgled and cried out, inhaling his first breath of life. His face flushed with color.

Filled with relief, I helped to dry the child. He had lived. At the same time I was deeply sad. If my sister Annie had lived, she would now have a baby as well.

Beaming, Som-kway passed the baby to Suk-ee-loon-gawn for her to hold. "When a child is born, it is our future," she told me.

Mother also loved babies. She did not believe, as most others did, that children were born into a sinful state or that midwives were often in league with Satan. If there was no minister nearby, Mother baptized the babies herself.

I prayed over this baby silently. *I baptize you in the name of the Holy Spirit.*

Mee-mun-dut, the Indians called him, which meant simply Baby. He would be named when he was a few years old.

The women laughed and danced about, hooting and cackling. They seemed to talk from their bellies rather than their mouths.

"He is beautiful! He is strong! He is healthy," Somkway shouted. She stomped one foot and yelled, *"Hoo! Hee-pa-ha!"*

What noise! If Puritans ever made such riotous merrymaking, they would be arrested, I thought. All behavior must be orderly and respectful.

Suk-ee-loon-gawn looked at her new son with a tenderness that surprised me. I turned to see Sa-kat's delighted, laughing eyes and the little space between her teeth when she smiled. I had to smile, too; for a moment I shared the good feeling and I saw clearly that the Indians, however strange, were capable of a joy that was rare among my own people.

The Gray Mare

AT THE END OF THE WINTER WAM-PAK returned with his warriors and declared that now, as the time for fishing and planting approached, the season of warfare had ended. Some of the warriors had been killed by the Dutch in the Wiechquaeskeck towns along the coast. Our village of a hundred now numbered about seventy-five. Elsewhere the losses were greater. Messengers reported that inland, at a place called Pound Ridge, the Dutch had slain five hundred Lenape Indians—Wappingers, Tankitke, and our own tribe, Siwanoy—by surrounding their houses with a ring of fire. I felt sick when I remembered my own family's house in flames. It seemed that the Indians might not win the war. Where would that leave me? Would the Dutch soldiers come to set me free? Would Thomas Cornell arrive with some of my brothers and sisters?

The women who mourned the lost warriors blackened their faces, tore out their hair, and cried pitifully for days. Wam-pak paced about the long house like a caged animal.

The last of the snow fell in large, round clusters.

Soon almost every bit of the snow had vanished. Spring was fast approaching.

One day Sa-kat and I followed Chah-kol and Tu-ma to the frozen river, where the boys had chopped holes for ice fishing. I traded glances with a codfish through the clear ice as the boys plunged in their spears. Tu-ma managed to catch the only fish that afternoon.

Serious fishing began as soon as the ice broke, and during the last chill of winter the bluefish moved into the sound. They swam northward to our own rocky inlet, where the boys and men of the village were ready for them with a giant circular fence made from saplings. As the tidewater withdrew, the fish lay stranded on the mud, to be killed with clubs. Then everyone in the village brought the fish back to the banks to gut them and hang them out to dry on lattices.

My feet sank into the ice-cold mud as I moved out toward the writhing bluefish. I stopped to watch one giant fish bite a hole in another.

"Look!" Chah-kol said. "They're so warlike, they sometimes eat one another!" I was surprised I could understand him. Every day, life in the village made a little more sense to me.

The next few weeks brought a raw, damp northeaster, so we moved the drying fish into our wigwams, living in the powerful smell. Several moonless, cloudy nights and days followed; the sound was calm and whispery, many shades of blue. At low tide we collected more fish. I didn't like to gut them and I despised watching them being clubbed to death. My brothers had used the much gentler method of making a sharp cut with a knife.

After many rains and storms the fishing season

ended. The ground thawed. Almost overnight the bare spots of clay and mud of the island turned to bright green marsh grass, and it was now time for planting corn.

As the trees reddened with buds and the first whorls of tiny leaves appeared, the women and girls laughed more easily. Some who had blackened their faces in grief in the winter now painted their cheeks with red circles. They paddled from the island to the planting ground, sometimes hooting with laughter. This made me angry. Though my Lenape was improving, I couldn't understand their jokes.

I let the others paddle for me, and I clutched the sides of the canoe because I would drown if the canoe overturned.

Once Sa-kat caught me staring at the swirling water.

"You don't know how to swim, do you?" she asked.

I frowned at her.

"I will teach you as soon as the water warms," she said.

"All right," I said, trying to disguise my fear.

In Boston the church had passed laws that no one could swim or dance, but Mother did not agree with those laws. I was sure that she would want me to swim so that I could save my own life.

A redheaded bird landed on a leafless bush. *"Pa-pa-hes,"* Sa-kat said.

As more new birds appeared in the woods every day, Sa-kat told me their names. Such noisy birds! Just like Sa-kat's constant chatter and pecking at me. I had become an Indian girl's little pet! I was almost as bound to her as the new baby was to Suk-ee-loon-gawn, strapped to his mother's back on a cradle board. I longed for afternoons with my sister Kate, practicing our handwriting with quill pens or playing with our rag dolls.

Readying the fields for planting was hard work. With our antler hoes we loosened the soil around each of the hills from the previous year and pulled up the dead plants by their thick roots. Som-kway was pleased that I knew how to rake the top of a corn hill flat with my hand. In the hill she planted a circle of seven kernels, six on the outside and one in the middle, before raking over the earth again.

I was supposed to work in Suk-ee-loon-gawn's group, but she said, "I don't want that salt person anywhere around me!"

"Wam-pak has adopted her. You must accept her," answered Som-kway.

"I hate you, Suk-ee-loon-gawn!" I said. I wished I knew the words in Lenape. I picked up a handful of dirt and threw it at her.

She threw dirt right back. We screamed at each other in our two languages until Som-kway stopped her.

It took about a month to plant, and Som-kway saw to it that Suk-ee-loon-gawn and I were separated. But in the long house I had to bear her insults.

After working in the cornfield, I usually spent the afternoons with Sa-kat and nine other children our own age. One day I followed them to the beach on the northern side of the island. There were enormous gray boulders, which the children liked to climb at low tide. I called one Gray Mare because it was shaped like a horse's head.

The boys climbed right up, followed by the girls. Sa-kat was not a natural climber, but she managed. I stood on the beach alone, looking up at the crowd of them high up there on the rock. I wanted to join in, but I was afraid. In my old world girls never did rough things like climb or hit the boys, as the Indians girls did.

Sa-kat called to me and waved. "Come join us!" she said.

Climbing was more difficult than it looked. I was still not used to my slippery new moccasins. The tide rose against the rock as I hoisted myself up. *There!*

Sa-kat congratulated me. We sat together, our hair blowing in the strong wind.

I looked around. Bordering the beach was a dense growth of green marsh grass that led to the woods. The turbulent water was deep blue. It was frightening to be up so high, but I was proud of myself. Finally I had done something the others could do.

The boys climbed down first, then the girls.

Climbing down the horse's head section of the rock would be easy enough, but between the neck and the base of the rock there was nowhere to grab hold. Water now lapped up to the other side of the rock. I had to jump quickly before the tide cut the rock off from land.

All the others had made it down to the bottom. They joked. *"Pah-see-aw-tum!"* They were calling me a half-wit.

Sa-kat tried to coax me down. But even she was laughing at me.

I yelled in English, "You people! You disgust me. I wish I had never come to live with you!"

A big wave broke on the water side of the rock. I crept down the opposite side, over the horse's head, then froze in fear.

Finally Chah-kol approached the rock. I could tell he was embarrassed.

Chah-kol had a slight, well-boned face and a bouncy gait. When he grinned, lines appeared at the corners of his mouth. Chah-kol stood beside the rock and then made a cup with his hands so that I could put my foot there.

I slid down and Chah-kol helped me. I shook a little when I reached the ground.

"Thank you," I whispered.

Chah-kol joined the pack of children, and they laughed even harder. Sa-kat came to my side. "It wasn't difficult, was it?"

I would not let her near me for the rest of the day.

That night the rain fell on the long house and on the leaves outside. I felt cold and miserable. All of a sudden I clearly saw what was happening. I had played with the children; I had climbed their rock. Wasn't I siding with the people who had killed my mother? I had betrayed my own family!

If I didn't run away soon, I would become an Indian!

Escape

ONCE I HAD MADE UP MY MIND, I THOUGHT only of escape. I would find my way to my family's old settlement and look for our neighbors. If I traveled west across the swamps and meadows of the mainland, I might eventually find my home. There was a way by canoe, but I suspected there was also a way by foot. Indian paths laced this land. One of these paths must be the right one.

I hid these thoughts away from Sa-kat and let her teach me new words. But sometimes she searched my face unhappily, as if she knew I did not want to be her friend.

I took a knife, dried venison, and a skin bag full of water and buried them under a bush near our canoes on the mainland. One morning I paddled to the cornfield with a group of girls. When I stepped out of the canoe, I lagged behind the others. Then, once out of sight, I collected my hidden belongings and ran up the path.

Panting, I raced on until I was beyond the planting fields. I pushed my way through a towering wall of yellow reeds. Blood ran from scratches on my legs.

Briars slashed my arms. I marched through densely matted cord grass and came to mudflats, where walking was much easier. The tide was low, and egrets and herons waded in the shallow water. The mud was alive with fiddler crabs.

I walked along the mudflats for several hours, and I thought: *If either the Cornells or the Throckmortons are alive, then why haven't they come for me?* Perhaps they did not know I had survived. Or what if they were dead? The terrible question beat in my head. I had to know the answer.

The mudflats opened onto a river, and I followed its twists and turns westward on the bank. Was this the river the Indians had used to reach my family's farm? My feet hurt and my back ached, but I walked on. As the sun began to set I came upon a large fallen tree. I ate a little of the venison and drank about half the water I was carrying; I could get more water from the river. I rested that night on the dry hollow log, opening my eyes every few minutes to check if the Indians were searching for me.

When morning came, I was so hungry that I couldn't help eating most of the dried meat. I followed the river, gaining strength because I felt I was moving in the right direction. Soon I recognized the rising ground, fields, the brook, a muddy bank surrounding it.

My heart raced ahead, but I forced myself to walk more slowly. I was afraid of missing the place, and I was afraid of finding it.

I walked into the fields, and the old terror rose up in me.

The house was gone.

My legs felt shaky. I was hot, so I removed my fur, then shivered when I remembered the way Wam-pak had struck my mother, how the dogs had barked, how everyone had screamed.

Why had I wanted to come? Everything familiar was curiously out of place. The creek was there, but not the barn. I'd expected cinders where the buildings had been. There were no bodies, no skeletons. Had they all vanished in the fire? I threw myself down and searched on all fours like an animal. Wasn't there one thing left to remind me of my family?

Oddly enough, the pasture was greener than ever. Red-winged blackbirds were building their nests in the tall grasses.

I remembered my mother standing tall, unafraid, arguing amidst frantic turmoil. I heard her hard, twangy voice. When she put us children to bed, her tone had always sweetened. She had still been hand-some, despite the years of struggle. I tried to remember her every gesture.

A leper, people called her. A Jezebel. An instrument of the devil. A woman who cavorted with the devil-snake. None of these things was true. Mother firmly trusted God. But why hadn't God delivered her?

I stared at the meadow, my heart pounding. I thought of Wam-pak, his hair in high, tufted ridges, his teeth in a crazy grin before he killed her. Shrieking and smoke from the burning barn filling the sky.

Now there was only the drone of insects. A feeling of peace lay across this meadow. How could that be?

What was that in the grass? It was a little boy's shoe, worn and moldy. I held it and brought it to my lips. It had been my little brother's shoe, the one he had lost when he ventured out into the meadow one day by himself. Poor Zuriel. He had been a small, eager child.

Why hadn't Mother listened to Will's warning?

I was too tired to move. I sat, my fur coat bunched around me, holding the shoe. Never wanting to see it again, I discarded it in the grass.

After a while I stood and looked about. The land on the far side of the hill seemed different to me. Mounds. What were they? *Graves.* I ran toward them with dread.

Eight graves, each marked by a stone. Mother, Annie, Will, Mary, Kate, William, Francis, and Zuriel. I cried out. Then I shouted, "They're all gone. Couldn't you have spared one of them, Lord? Kate? Mother?"

I fingered the markers. Then I gathered yellow and purple wildflowers and left them as offerings. *God bless them,* I prayed. *God be with them all.* I said, "Mother, forgive me for being angry with you when you died. I wish . . . to live my life . . . in such a way as to make you proud."

Who had buried my family? Who had put those markers there?

Help must be nearby, if I could only find it.

It was a long walk to the Throckmorton settlement. By the time I got there, the sky was streaked red and orange.

The houses were gone, though one barn was left standing. Again I felt that terrible chill pass through me as I counted the graves. Seventeen. About two dozen people had lived here. So it seemed that a few had gotten away.

My family had lived here with the Cornells and Throckmortons before our house was finished. I remembered the warmth and happiness that had swept over Rebecca Cornell's face when my family first came to her home. She was so grateful to have new neighbors. She set out pewter mugs and spoons; she fed us every food she had with a shining trust. Mother did not want to live with the other families; she did not want John Throckmorton or anyone else to tell us what to do. But after we moved to our own house, we had sometimes taken the long walk to visit and do our chores together. I had liked to dip candles or stir a kettle of lye soap with the other girls.

I approached the barn cautiously. Why hadn't the Indians burned it? I called out, trembling. I flipped the latch and opened the door. There was nothing inside. I sat for several moments, totally alone. I lay down on my back. Soon I fell fast asleep.

The next morning the cold woke me. The wind outside was harsh. I covered myself with the hay and slept, though insects bit me.

I dreamed of Boston and of the day when Mother had walked out of the meetinghouse one Sunday morning in the middle of the service. Our services lasted four hours. The small frame meetinghouse had been freezing cold. We had to sit still and straight, boys and men on the right, girls and women on the left, listening to Reverend Cartwright's inexhaustible talk and wheezing.

I had been seated between Mother and Kate, near the end of the row, holding Kate's hand. I was wearing my yellow woolen gown with the white linen collar, a hand-me-down from Kate. I was too young to understand Reverend Cartwright's talk of hell and damnation.

But Mother was at the edge of her bench, keenly listening. "We'll all sit till doomsday under legal sermons and never see the light. Come, girls," she whispered to me and my sisters. Mother stood up, startling the whole church. Chin high, she marched down the center aisle. She always moved with dignity. Then, one by one, we followed: Kate and I, Faith, Bridget, Annie, and Mary.

I had glanced over at my father and my brothers on the other side of the meetinghouse as we walked by. My elder brothers, Edward and Richard, were pink with embarrassment. Some of the boys around them were snickering. Father, as usual, looked at us with pain and sympathy. Perhaps he had had a feeling of what the future would bring.

When I woke at dawn the day was gray and cold. I drank some water from the brook and filled my skin bag. "Mother," I said, "what would you have me do now?"

The only answer was the gentle flowing sound of the brook. It seemed to say, "Keep going."

There was a Dutch fort in New Amsterdam, within a few days' walk. Perhaps the people there would know how to contact my brothers and sisters in Narragansett and Boston. I remembered my family saying the fort lay to the south of the farm, on Manhattan Island. Would I be able to find it? And if so, would the Dutch take in an English girl?

I ate my last few pieces of meat and followed the river onward.

The Bear

By the end of the day I realized that the trees I had seen that morning looked like the same trees I'd seen that afternoon.

I sank down on my knees. I must have been going in circles. The river did not go south to Manhattan Island but twisted and turned back on itself. I was lost.

That night I slept in an old ruined canoe, shivering from the wet and cold. I had not found anything to eat for the whole day. My stomach growled. I was hungrier than I had ever been in my life, and so exhausted I could hardly move. But I had to find the fort!

I woke the next morning too tired to sit up. A great horned owl swooped above me and disappeared. I decided to rest for a while. The weather was colder than the day before. My feet were wet and chilled. The wind whipped my hair.

I remembered the taste of my mother's stew and how good it smelled cooking. Then I remembered the taste of the Indians' warm venison dipped in maple sugar. I pictured the Indians in their long house, scooping *sa-pan* into their mouths with clamshells. Even if there wasn't always meat, Som-kway had sweet-tasting mush ready for the taking at any time of day or night. . . .

No. The Indians had killed my family.

But Sa-kat . . . how patiently she had taught me.

Wam-pak, grinning with his terrible teeth. How could I even think of living with him again?

Som-kway had always looked at me tenderly with her dark eyes and wrinkled face.

My thoughts bounced back and forth. Would the Indians take me back? If they wanted me, why hadn't they come for me?

How would I survive without food and shelter?

The Indians were my enemies. Were they also my only hope of survival?

What choice did I have? I did not feel at all decided, but with my last bit of strength, I chose to follow the river in hope of finding Place of Stringing Beads village. Perhaps, if I was lucky, I would find myself at the fort instead.

As I plodded on, I remembered Kate. Then I thought of Sa-kat. In many ways she had been like a sister.

How would the Dutch treat me? Would strangers at the fort treat me better than the Indians had? I thought of the sad look Sa-kat occasionally had when I disappointed her. Surely she was missing me now.

By afternoon my shoulders stooped. My back ached. Light rain fell from the sky. I came to a place bordered by the woods. There I'd have shelter from the rain. The woods were wet and green and smelled of budding trees.

A dark figure emerged from a clump of patchy bushes. I gasped. A bear!

I stood motionless as I breathed in its musky, rank odor. The bear rose until it stood upright, its massive head turning toward me. It fixed me in its yellow eyes.

Lord, help me, I prayed. Then I noticed a big oak tree with a low branch. I jumped toward it and climbed, shaking. I scrambled higher.

The bear ran to the tree. I was just out of his reach. The bear growled and clawed the tree. Then, abruptly, he looked at me as if there were an understanding between us. I stared deep into the yellow eyes.

By some miracle Wam-pak appeared. He saw me but kept silent because of the bear. We looked at each other; the snake on his forehead stood still. The bear did not notice him at first. The only sound was the rain falling on the leaves. Then Wam-pak's two dogs rushed up, barking furiously. The bear turned.

Wam-pak drew back his bow and struck the bear's side. His arrow fell away as the bear snarled and showed its great pointed teeth.

Wam-pak rushed forward, jabbing with his spear. The bear clawed his hand. Wam-pak tripped and fell on top of the bear. Wam-pak, the dogs, and the bear rolled together. Wam-pak made a desperate lunge and struck the bear's heart with a knife.

Wam-pak stood. "The bear is dead. Come." In angry silence I climbed down from the tree with shaking legs. Wam-pak steadied me as blood dripped from his hand. He offered a prayer for the soul of the bear, then turned to me.

"Mee-pahk, you will return with me."

I hit him. "I hate you!" I said in English. He stood still and looked at me.

I had no choice! No choice but to go with him. I

knew I would give in, but I didn't want him to know it. Why did he want me? I hit him again and I felt a bit better, even relieved.

"Come," he said. We started to walk, and the dogs ran ahead.

"You killed my mother!" I said in Lenape.

After a pause Wam-pak began to talk as we walked together slowly. "Our people used to trade with the white people," he said, "but there had been trouble. The white men sold our people liquor, then stole our furs and took our lands. Once one of our warriors killed a white man because his cattle wandered into our field and destroyed our corn. Then a white man gave our people a deadly sickness. More than half of our people perished. My wife and daughter died. But this was not the cause of the war."

Wam-pak stopped to see how I would take his words.

"You killed my family!" I choked out.

Wam-pak held his back stiffly straight and went on. "The white chief at the fort sent men to us with their weapons of fire. They took our corn. They would not sell the Lenape guns, but on the great river to the north, they sold guns to our enemies the Iroquois. This left us without defense. One night a powerful band of the Iroquois, the Mohawks, traveled down the river to make war with our fellow Lenape, the Wiechquaeskeck.

"The Wiechquaeskeck asked for help from the white people at the fort. The leader of the fort sheltered them. Then, after a few days, the white men crept up and killed them in their sleep. The fort's leader displayed our people's heads on poles. This is why all warriors of our tribes are fighting the white men. This is why your family was killed."

I stopped breathing for a moment. There was a long silence. I listened to the wet leaves on the trees rustling in the wind. "My mother and my brothers and sisters did your people no harm." I exploded in a fit of crying.

"My people are at war with your people," Wam-pak answered.

"My people are English. You are at war with the Dutch."

Wam-pak was silent. I didn't know if he understood me or not.

"Why didn't you kill me with the others?"

"I brought you to be a daughter. To be a sister to my other daughter."

After that we walked together in silence.

Mercy

WHEN WE APPEARED IN PLACE OF STRINGING Beads village, Som-kway was sitting cross-legged on the rushes of our long house, her cheeks oddly flushed.

Wam-pak held his clawed hand awkwardly. *"Mah-kwa,"* he said triumphantly, telling them of the bear.

Sa-kat looked as if she was about to burst into tears.

Tobacco smoke hung heavily in the air. This meant that Som-kway had been praying and chanting to the spirits. She greeted me brusquely. I gave her an apologetic look.

Suk-ee-loon-gawn met me with scornful silence.

It was an empty and remorseful evening for me. As hungry as I was, it was difficult to eat. The air in the long house seemed heavy; the small room was full of unspoken emotion. I breathed in the sharp tobacco smell. As we sat and Som-kway fed me, Sa-kat gave me a preoccupied, brooding look. It would take some time for her to tell me what she thought. As was the custom of the Indians, she must follow the example of the leader, Som-kway. Would the family once again accept me? Now I cared whether they did or not.

It took four men to bring the bear back to the is-

66

land. Som-kway opened the bear and took out its heart and liver. She wrapped them in fat and put them on an open spit. The next day a ceremony followed.

"*Hoo!*" Wam-pak shouted.

"*Ka-yah!*" the people answered with shouts of joy. The drumming began.

Som-kway gave me a look that was still angry.

I let my hair cover my eyes and watched the men dance around the carcass of the bear.

Som-kway took her younger brother, Mah-kwa, the medicine man, aside from the dance. I strained to hear their whispers.

"The girl ran away," Som-kway said to her brother, her wrinkled face puckered. "We must kill her. Yet Wam-pak refuses."

Kill me! I almost cried out.

"Wam-pak tells us that it was she who brought the bear to us," Mah-kwa said. "He says the girl has remarkable gifts. She knew how to look at the bear and make him still."

Som-kway talked without emotion. "Wam-pak is inventing excuses. It would not please me to see the girl die, yet we must follow the laws of our people. This is an ugly matter. I fault Wam-pak. It is not so simple to take a captive of her age and expect her to become one of us."

"Perhaps she will bring us luck. She brought the bear."

"More likely she will bring us trouble. Suk-ah-sun died because of her. The white men from the fort may come looking for her one of these days."

"Then she will be valuable. Protection from another terrible attack. Even more of a reason to let her live."

All my strength seemed to rush out of me. *Let me live,* I prayed.

Som-kway returned to the festivities. As the boys and men danced, she talked in an eerie singsong way. Her teeth were huge and yellow. It had not been Som-kway who saved my life but Wam-pak. Who were my friends? Who were my enemies?

The spirit of the bear seemed to rise out of the music. Skinned, it looked almost human. A bear, of all the animals, resembled a man when its fur was removed.

I looked over at Sa-kat and found that she was still eyeing me with nervous sorrow. She showed no interest or pleasure in the festivities. I felt more alone than ever, but I tried to stand straight and hold my shoulders back.

Behind me someone shook a rattle, a turtle shell filled with pebbles.

Now Wam-pak rested from dancing. He took a step toward me. His injured hand was wrapped in skins. "Mee-pahk, I want you to have the bearskin. It is an honor to have a bearskin."

"Thank you," I said. It was the first time I had said that to him. I was not happy or unhappy, but suspended somewhere in between. Wam-pak clearly did not mean to harm me, despite what he had done to my family. Oddly enough, he was my ally. He had come to my defense when Som-kway had not. These things made no sense to me.

Som-kway approached. She looked grave. I had no idea what would come next.

"Mee-pahk, I know life is not easy for you. You have seen more pain than is good for you. At the same time, you must realize you are part of a community here. You must follow our ways if you are to live with us."

My hands extended in a gesture of helplessness.

"I understand you," I said meekly.

Som-kway opened her arms to me in a hearty embrace. She studied my face closely. There was no guile in her eyes.

"It is our custom to kill those who run away," she said, and I shuddered. "But it is Wam-pak's wish that we accept you as a daughter."

I stared into her eyes.

"You have all the blessings of the heavens, Mee-pahk. Wam-pak is the warrior chief of our people and I am the spiritual leader. If we accept you, the others will follow."

"I will try to work harder in the tasks that you give me," I said.

Som-kway grinned. "You are a good girl. Now eat!"

Sa-kat came to me and took my hand. We looked at each other and smiled shyly. I was one with the Lenape again, even if some members of the tribe treated me with scorn.

Over the next days Som-kway showed me how to scrape the bear hide with a sharp stone scraper and smear it with the bear's brain to preserve it. When the skin was ready, she allowed me to take it into the long house to my own sleeping platform.

A bear-fur cloak was something only a few Lenape children possessed. I accepted it with gratitude and remorse. In an odd way the bear's death had made it possible for me to be allowed back into the village. Still, I wished that the bear had lived—even though, like Wam-pak, it might have killed me.

The Merman

MY CONVERSATIONS WITH SA-KAT THAT SPRING were easier, and we were able to talk about more substantial things. Outside the long house one day, making a stew of squirrel, corn, beans, and sunflower seeds, I dared to ask her the questions that were on my mind.

"Is Wam-pak your father?" I asked.

"Yes," she said.

"Is Suk-ee-loon-gawn your mother?"

"She is my mother, though she is the sister of the woman who gave birth to me."

"I don't understand," I said.

"She who gave birth to me is now in the world with the spirits. She walks the path of the stars in the sky."

"Isn't Mee-kwun your brother?"

"Mee-kwun and Mee-mun-dut are my brothers." She nodded.

A shocking picture unfolded as Sa-kat continued to explain.

Wam-pak had married two sisters at the same time. One sister, who had died, had been the mother of Sa-kat. The other sister, Suk-ee-loon-gawn, had given birth to a daughter, who had also died. Suk-ee-loon-gawn was the mother of two sons, Mee-kwun and the baby, Mee-mun-dut.

"My sister is gone, and now *you* are my new sister. You take her place!" Sa-kat said.

I was certainly *not* Sa-kat's sister, but nothing would have convinced her otherwise.

The conversation ended as Suk-ee-loon-gawn came along and scooped herself a bowlful of the stew. It was like Suk-ee-loon-gawn to arrive whenever the food was ready. I looked at her with a new sense. Suk-ee-loon-gawn hated me because I was meant to take the place of her daughter, killed by a disease that white people had brought. I felt a spark of sympathy for her.

In the days that followed, I thought about Sa-kat's lost sister. The names of the dead were never uttered among the Indians. When I was alone with Sa-kat, I asked her the name. She refused to tell me, though once she drew a picture of a flower in the sand. The girl's name, I supposed, was See-pu-neh-kway, Water Lily Woman.

I looked up at Sa-kat's sad face. She was so pretty! She had a generous, glorious head of hair. Mine was thin and lank. She also carried herself with dignity, and she was frank and intelligent.

Sa-kat combed my hair with a bone comb. She did so energetically and lovingly, as my sisters had. She tied it with a string laced with small seashells. I patted my hair. "Oh, thank you!" I cried, and she smiled at me in delight. For some reason I felt tears in my eyes.

We walked together on the beach, and the cool wind blew from the water.

"Is Som-kway Suk-ee-loon-gawn's mother? Or Wam-pak's mother?" I asked.

"Suk-ee-loon-gawn's," she answered. "A man moves into the home of his wife's mother when he marries."

More mysteries unfolded as I was able to understand Sa-kat's words.

"Som-kway is a *mu-teh-kway*," she told me, "a medicine woman. Maybe I too will become a medicine woman one day."

So that was why Som-kway collected roots and leaves to make strange pastes. My mother also knew how to make salves and medicines; she had learned as a little girl in England. I wished she'd had the time to teach me.

Sa-kat did not understand much when I told her about Mother's troubles with the clergy, but she understood about witches and witchcraft.

"There *is* a witch in our village," she said. "I'd stay away from Noo-chee-hu-weh-kway. You do not yet know all our ways, so you would be easy prey to her!"

Mother had believed that most women who were accused of witchcraft were innocent. But Mother had never said that witches did not exist. Were any of the Lenape in a pact with the devil?

I soon met Noo-chee-hu-weh-kway, Witch Woman. She lived at the opposite end of the village. She seemed ordinary enough except for the penetrating expression of her eyes. Would she cast a spell on me? I decided to keep a close watch on Som-kway as well, just in case.

• • •

One day Sa-kat took me to sit on a pile of rocks on the north side of our island, near the Gray Mare. She shook the dirt and pebbles out of her moccasins. At a distance a group of gulls stood in a row on the gray rocks, watching us.

"Mee-pahk, now, before the tide comes in, I'm going to teach you how to swim."

Lord, protect me, I said silently.

Following her example, I stripped off my clothes in a way that would have horrified me several months earlier. I no longer felt so shy, at least not around Sa-kat. I was learning not to feel ashamed of my body, like Sa-kat. We walked over the mud, avoiding the slime-covered rocks, and into the blue-gray water. We waded in a little farther. The water felt icy cold.

When the water covered my waist, I lowered myself in, holding on to Sa-kat. While she stood, I grasped her shoulders tightly and kicked my legs. I sank and choked. "Don't worry," she said, and pulled me up. "Don't be afraid." I trembled and bit my lower lip. "Let's try again," she said. This time I did not sink.

Soon Tu-ma and Chah-kol came by in a dugout canoe full of clams.

"Your white bottom is showing!" Tu-ma called.

"Go away!"

"White bottom! White bottom!" the brothers called.

"Pimply face! That's you!" Sa-kat answered.

I ducked down into the water.

Sa-kat taught me to swim each day at low tide.

A thought occurred to me once when I was practicing. "Would you ever marry Tu-ma or Chah-kol?"

"You silly goose!" she said. "Tu-ma and Chah-kol are our cousins. They're Turtles, like us. We can only marry boys who are of the Wolf or Turkey clans."

"Good," I replied, remembering that each hut in the

village was marked with one of the three clan symbols. "Chah-kol and Tu-ma are such pests!"

"Yes, pests," she said. "They are just alike, two little weasels! Now, show me you can swim by yourself. Don't be afraid. You are going to have to get used to it."

I shut my eyes, then leaped forward, kicking and thrashing. *"Hoo! Eh-chay-tam-way!"* she cried.

Beaming, I rose from the water. I had done it!

• • •

The corn plants grew tall, with the beans, squash, and pumpkins winding around them. About every four days we weeded the corn hills, but we didn't bother to check on the corn otherwise. There was time now to paddle with the other children to an island we called Place of Seashells, south of our island, and return with canoes full of clams, mussels, and oysters. As they dried in the sun and their shells opened, we pulled out their meat and threw it into the cooking pots.

The corn would not ripen for some time, and the men did not hunt big game, yet we feasted. Often the men took their nets, woven and weighted with stones, and hurled them at the geese and ducks to capture them. All feathers, the ducks proved difficult to clean.

Not far from the cornfield, feeding into Turtle Cove, was a small round pond.

"The *wew-too-na-wes* lives here," Sa-kat said ominously.

"What kind of sea monster?" I asked.

"He has a flipper instead of legs."

"Have you seen him yourself?"

"No. He hasn't appeared for quite some time, but

we know he's down there. That's why we don't swim in the pond. Once a few years ago the merman grabbed a little boy by the legs and pulled him under. He was never seen again! His body didn't surface!"

I didn't think I believed in the merman, but I thought of the boy whenever we walked past the place. That summer Tu-ma spotted two small turtles sitting on a log at the far end of the pond. "Who wants to get them?" he dared.

"I'm going to catch one of them and make a new rattle," Chah-kol said.

"Don't go out there," Sa-kat warned.

At that moment I pictured a giant snapping turtle just under the surface of the water. "Come back!" I called.

Chah-kol ventured out on the log.

"Come back!" I called again.

"Get that turtle!" Tu-ma said.

Suddenly Chah-kol made a lunge at one of the turtles. Both leaped into the pond with a splash. Then Chah-kol lost his balance and fell in.

Chah-kol cheerfully swam toward us. "It's nice to cool off!" he said.

"Get out right now." Sa-kat was almost in tears.

Chah-kol continued to paddle about. "Tu-ma, why don't you join me?" he asked. Then he cried out. "My foot! Something's got my foot!"

Chah-kol's head disappeared under the water with a jerk, then resurfaced again. "Help!"

Tu-ma dove in, grabbed hold, and pulled him to shore. Soon the boys stood on the shore of the pond, soaking wet and dripping. Blood ran from a bite on Chah-kol's foot.

"It was the *wew-too-na-wes*!" Chah-kol said. He wiped the blood from his foot with some leaves.

"What did the *wew-too-na-wes* look like?" Sa-kat asked.

"I don't know, but I think he's very big!" Chah-kol answered.

As we all walked through the swamp on the way back to our canoes, I thought of the snapping turtle. I had seen it clearly in my mind. How had I known it was there?

The Wolf Cubs

THE MOUNDS OF EMPTY SHELLS NEAR OUR village grew into small mountains. The men took some of the clamshells to fashion pretty purple-and-white beads called *wampum*. Of all the younger boys, Tu-ma worked at the beads with the most interest and diligence. I watched him break the shells into little pieces, then work them back and forth in the grooves of a grindstone until they were smooth and round. He perforated them with an iron drill that had come from a trade with Dutch settlers. The boys and men chipped spear points and arrowheads as well, some long and others broad, from the gray stone they found near the river.

The men taught the boys to make canoes. They chose tulip trees, tall and straight and almost branchless except for the tops, and burned rings around their bases to make the felling easier. They built fires in the logs. Then they scraped out the ashes with adzes and mallets. At both ends of each log, one of the more experienced men would take a stone chisel and wooden mallet to carefully chip and shape the canoe's pointed bow and stern.

"Can I help?" I asked.

"No, this is boys' work!" Chah-kol answered.

Chah-kol's and Tu-ma's beginning efforts were clumsy.

"What a stinker! I don't see how this canoe will ever float!" I was beginning to learn how to joke, like the Lenape.

"It's going to sink right down to the bottom, where the merman is waiting for it!" Sa-kat added.

"It will float, all right," Chah-kol said.

The boys worked day after day. They talked of taking long journeys together as soon as they were a bit older and were permitted to leave the community.

Chah-kol grinned at me, lines appearing at the corners of his mouth. "You are such a baby, Mee-pahk, but I see that you need a canoe. I'm going to give you mine."

"He's giving you a precious gift," Sa-kat told me.

I couldn't believe Chah-kol had been so generous! The Lenape children were like this.

The first time I pushed the canoe into the water and glided out over the clear, stony bottom, I felt an unguarded joy I had never felt before. The water sparkled in the sunlight. I scanned the maze of ducks in the lagoon: some tufted, some green, others black and white. The lagoon was filled with so many ducks that if you looked at them from a distance, they seemed like specks of dirt or hundreds of rocks. They flew up like a storm and filled the sky like dark clouds.

The boat was heavy. I followed the other children in their canoes. Outside the lagoon the currents were stronger and I spun around in circles.

"You silly girl! The dwarves have taken your mind

and are playing tricks on you," Sa-kat said. She laughed with her soft brown eyes. How poised she was in her own canoe.

"What dwarves?"

"The *wem-ah-tay-ku-nees-uk,* or the all-over-the-woods creatures, are magical people about three feet high who live in the forest," Sa-kat explained. "These little people are tricky! You must watch out for them!"

I was not as good a paddler as the others. I grew tired, my hands blistered, and my back was uncomfortable. Still, there was nothing I would rather have done than paddle.

It was summertime, my third season with the Lenape. The weather became so muggy that the children and I played in the water for days at a stretch. I loved to swim, and we were too hot and lazy to do anything else. I had forgotten that sloth was sinful; this simple life of play suited me. We swam most of the day. Then we paddled to the nearby Place of Seashells to collect clams and mussels, and we boiled them for our evening meal. The Lenape seemed so healthy. They took to the water easily, as though their short, broad paddles were extensions of themselves. There was an unmistakable air of pleasure about them, unlike my own family's soberness. It was odd for people to paint their faces, yet it suited them. Soon my skin freckled, burned, peeled, then darkened. I had become less modest about covering my chest.

I was surprised that no adults cared if we remained outside after dark. We once canoed well past sunset, the full moon shining on the water. We stayed on the Place of Seashells all night, around a campfire. I grew afraid as Chah-kol told scary stories. Then, in the distance, I heard a child loudly shrieking.

"What was that?" I asked.

No one else had heard it. Again a scream pierced the cool air, but this time it sounded more like a woman's voice.

"I heard someone scream!" I said.

"It was the Silent Walker, the witch!" Sa-kat answered. "You heard her first. Perhaps she is sending thoughts to your mind. She may be after you!"

While the others slept, I worried about the witch. I lay stiff all night until the sun rose and the geese honked loudly over our heads.

• • •

One day the children dared each other to go down into the wolf den, not far from our cornfield. The wolf pack usually roamed the forest, but it stayed in one place at this time of year to rear the cubs.

The den was cut into a small hill and went deep down into the earth. During the day some of the adult wolves left the den to go off and hunt. Surrounding the den were clumps of feathers and old bones.

"Who wants to go first?" Kee-tak asked. This nickname was a shortened form that meant He Is Heard Nearby. He always spoke loudly and authoritatively.

Tu-ma disappeared down into the wolf den. A few minutes later he emerged, his small brow covered with sweat. All the Lenape children took their turns, and soon it was mine.

"There is nothing to fear, Mee-pahk," one of the boys told me. "Wolves won't hurt us." The Lenape had a special admiration for wolves because they lived together in packs peacefully and took turns caring for their young.

"Here's the torch," Tu-ma said.

This was my chance to prove to the group that I was one of them. I took a deep breath and crawled down into the hole headfirst, feeling my way along.

The tunnel bent to the left and then to the right. It smelled sharply of urine. I pushed my way past some old bones and tufts of shredded fur.

The den opened up into a small room. Six orange-and-buff-colored cubs, curled into balls, lifted their heads to look at me. Their eyes shone red at me in the torchlight. Their paws were half as large as my hands.

One wolf cub growled at me and showed me its sharp teeth. My heart raced. I turned around and crawled out of the den as fast as I could.

"You look like you've just seen the merman," Chah-kol said.

Everyone laughed. The boys hooted and slapped their thighs. We started to walk away from the den as a wolf with a mottled coat emerged from the wood and trotted in our direction.

"It's the mother wolf. Don't run," Tu-ma warned. "If we stay still, she will not hurt us."

The mother wolf began to move past us. Then the wolf turned and slowly walked directly toward me. She stopped near my feet; she was so close that I could almost feel her soft fur. I held my breath, feeling numb, strangely weak. Without using words, I tried to tell the wolf not to attack me. I told her that we meant no harm. The wolf sniffed at the air curiously. She looked at me with her round, yellow-brown eyes. Then she disappeared into the den and surfaced again with all six wolf cubs.

The furry cubs walked around on their enormous feet. The cubs had smaller ears and shorter noses than the adults. The mother wolf licked some of the cubs. They nosed the corner of her mouth. Then she regurgitated the food in her stomach, and the wolf cubs ate it hungrily.

Three more wolves ran out of the woods. One carried the bloodied carcass of a baby doe. The wolves stood over the carcass.

I was quivering, too stunned to think what to do next. Everyone trembled now, even the boys.

"No one run," Tu-ma whispered. "If we run, they will attack us."

The wolves played with each other, nuzzling and sniffing. One wagged its tail. They rubbed noses with the large wolf that had brought in the kill, and licked its face.

One wolf pup playfully tugged on an adult's tail.

I took hold of Sa-kat's hand.

"It's all right. They have the doe to eat. They won't bother us," Sa-kat said, her voice cracking. I felt soothed.

"Everyone, we can leave now; but go slowly, don't run," Kee-tak said.

"Did you see how the she-wolf acted toward you?" Chah-kol said to me. "Mee-pahk, you have a talent with animals!"

Slowly, single file, we walked away from the wolves. When the path opened up to the shore and our canoes were in sight, we started to run.

Illness and Vision

AS WE HARVESTED THE CORN THAT FALL, I
began to think that I would never find a way to get to
my family. A year had passed and no one had come to
rescue me. My little pile of stones to count the days had
scattered long ago, but I could tell by the chill in the air
that I was now eleven.

Soon the men would go off to war. The boys I
played with were still too young to be warriors, but
their time would come.

One day I washed clothes with the girls from the
village, beating the skins and furs against the rocks and
letting them dry in the sun. My attention was caught by
a masked figure moving in the woods, a large, hunched
man in glossy bear furs. His mask was painted red on
the right side and black on the left.

"It's Mu-sing!" Som-kway called out. "Everyone,
find some gifts to give him! Quickly!"

He waddled out of the brush. Then he raised both
feet at once in a hip-hop motion. He carried a pointed
stick in one hand, and in the other he held a rattle
made from the shell of a snapping turtle.

I cringed at the earsplitting *crack* as the man shook the rattle.

Som-kway quickly held out some shells and handed them to him. Suk-ee-loon-gawn took off one of her necklaces. The masked figure slipped them into a deerskin sack he wore over his shoulders.

I put my hands over my ears as the gruesome figure lunged toward me and shook the rattle. I came face-to-face with the ugly mask, its crooked smile frozen in a grin and its forehead wrinkled in rows of black V-shaped lines.

Everything grew blurry, and then the world started to spin. I slumped to the ground. When I woke up, I was lying in the long house covered by my bearskin, with Som-kway and Sa-kat standing over me. They looked worried.

"Rest awhile. I will bring you some broth," Som-kway said, and stepped outside.

"Who was that?" I asked Sa-kat.

"It was Mu-sing. He is the spirit who is in charge of the wild animals and who gives game to the hunters. He rides around the forest on the back of a deer."

Mu-sing meant Living Solid Face. Was it a spirit or an ordinary man?

"I don't understand."

"He comes to remind us of the *gamwing* ceremony," Sa-kat answered. "You're going to like the Big House ceremony, Mee-pahk. Last year you were not permitted into the *gamwing* until you were adopted by the tribe. This year you'll participate more. The ceremony's going to last for twelve days, and there will be a lot of feasting. I know how you like to eat! Som-kway says that though you're not accomplished like the Lenape, you do two things very well: talking and eating!"

"Praise indeed," I said, feigning anger.

"Here, I want to show you something." She ran over to her sleeping platform and returned with a new deer-skin skirt decorated with purple porcupine quills and hanging bits of red-dyed deer fur. She held the lovely skirt to her body. "Suk-ee-loon-gawn made it for me for the ceremony."

I took the skirt and stood up. I had risen too quickly, however. I sank down to my knees, dizzy and hot.

"Lie down," Som-kway said, bringing in a bowl full of steaming broth.

She put down the broth and helped me back onto the sleeping platform. She felt my forehead. "The fever is rising again."

She held the bowl of broth while I drank from it. "Drink slowly." Suddenly I felt nauseated and vomited up the broth.

"Sa-kat, put that skirt away and help me clean up the mess this girl has made. She's ill. We must chase away the evil spirits."

Feeling wretched, I fell in and out of sleep. Some-times I'd open my eyes to find the family all looking at me. Soon I was aware that it was dark and that they slept. Then at dawn, Som-kway took me to the mud hut filled with the steam of heated rocks. Naked, I sweated and shivered. She led me to the beach and plunged me into the water, as she had done before the villagers had adopted me. Som-kway made me repeat this several times, until I begged her to stop.

Som-kway wrapped me in a light deerskin cloak and bade me lie down on the floor of the long house on my bearskin near one of the fires. She gave me some water but no food. She asked me to turn over on my stomach. I felt the fingers of her wise, strong hands pressing into my back. She synchronized her breath with mine, bearing into me with each new exhalation. Then she moved along my legs, pressing her palms into me, chasing my aches and cramps from one place to another.

When Som-kway was finished, I turned over and gazed at the masses of hanging corn, braided together and dangling from the rafters.

"Do you feel any better?" Som-kway asked.

"Yes, a little," I said. "Why is the fever doing a hopping dance around my body?"

"The sickness will not leave you. It's not ready," she answered matter-of-factly.

Som-kway shifted position. She sat with her knees close to me. Then she rocked me gently while she sang a low, mournful song.

One of the dogs came and licked my face.

"Get away!" I pushed it from me.

Then, prompted by Som-kway's singing, the dog began to howl.

I laughed at the dog. I was feeling warm and relaxed, dreamy and vague, but a little better. But just then I sat up, alarmed, as a man wearing a wolfskin headdress, its nose and ears and snout all dyed red, rushed in through the back door. He hunched over me and shook a small turtle-shell rattle. The man had pointy wolf fangs in his mouth.

I screamed and rushed to the corner, kicking over one of the cooking pots.

The man in the wolfskin sang a long incantation. I did not recognize the words, but I did recognize the voice. It was Mah-kwa. I realized then that the Mu-sing had also been Mah-kwa. I felt a bit relieved, though my heart still pounded fast inside me.

"Enough!" Som-kway scolded. The man retreated somewhere into the darkness.

In the next few days and nights I was aware of people coming and going. Tossing and turning and shaking from chills, I was only vaguely conscious of Som-kway leaning over me, wiping my face, and giving me her concoctions.

In a dream I found myself standing alone near Turtle Pond, where Chah-kol had fallen. On the grass near the shore was a big snapping turtle. He was dark green, very old, ugly, maimed in some way. He dragged himself along. Without using human words, he told me that he would lie in wait at the bottom of the pond for food. He had once lived in another pond, where the water wasn't so muddy and where there had been more fish.

"You did it to me!" the turtle accused me.

"What did I do?" I asked.

"You brought me here."

Scrapes and cuts marked the animal's carapace. I had never met this turtle, though he seemed familiar to me. Why was he talking to me like this?

"You let people cut me up!" the snapping turtle went on. "Many people hurt me."

"Who hurt you?" I asked, but the turtle just continued to complain.

I had another dream, of a big white swan. It slipped out of my heart, and I laughed because it was so big. It flapped its great feathery wings. The feathers tickled me. The bird alighted on the grassy ground south of Turtle Pond. The swan allowed me to pat its wings. With it, I knew I could fly. Like a swan, I stretched out my neck and put my arms out to my sides. I rose up with the swan, above the trees and water.

We circled around the Place of Seashells. From the air, it was a long, thin, wooded island surrounded by rocky beaches. Then we circled around Place of Stringing Beads island and nearby Two Island, gliding down and soaring through the narrow lagoon that separated them. We flew in closer to see the village, and nearby, on the beach, all the people of the village cutting and drying fish. Suk-ee-loon-gawn, Som-kway, and Sa-kat were there, baking fish in a rock shelter. Then the swan and I flew up and out, over the mainland again, over the cornfields and marshes, to where my family's house had stood, at the highest point of the meadow. I shuddered.

"Don't be afraid. I am with you," the swan said, and I saw that there was nothing to fear. The air was still and full of buzzing mosquitoes. It was late morning. The last wildflowers of the summer were beginning to fade.

We rose in flight again and circled around to a rocky crag near Twin Island. A large family of swans huddled on these rocks.

The swans seemed familiar to me. I knew somehow that the swans were the spirits of all my family members who had died.

"Mother, where are you?" I asked. But the birds were silent, their bodies folded. They did not talk in words, but they indicated they knew and loved me.

"Pretty swan . . . Turtle, go away. He won't stop

coming back. It's that snapping turtle," I muttered. Through a dim and restless sleep, I sensed someone beside me. I opened my eyes. Som-kway was studying me with interest.

"Tell me what you saw," she whispered.

"No." I stared at her. Had I received visions like Mother?

"I see it in your eyes that you have visited the spirits, Mee-pahk. You talked of a turtle. You spoke of a swan. You must tell me."

"I didn't see anything." I shook my head. But even though I was clearly awake, I could still see the turtle's red, slitty eyes looking at me with a sidelong glance.

"If any of the spirit animals remain with you now," Som-kway instructed, "tell them they may visit you again and that you are interested in hearing what they have to say. Thank them. Then bid them farewell."

The turtle began to behave better when I silently acknowledged him. He left the grass and slid back to the bottom of the pond.

The Telling
of the Dream

WHEN I WOKE AGAIN, SOM-KWAY HAD FETCHED
her brother, the medicine man Mah-kwa, who asked
me to tell him about my dreams.

"You must tell us, Mee-pahk," Mah-kwa said. "If we
do not heed what the spirits say, terrible things might
happen to you or to all of us!"

Som-kway had recognized I was something out of
the ordinary. I had not been able to hide it. I trembled
as I told Som-kway and Mah-kwa what I had seen.

Mah-kwa leaned against the wall of the long house,
his arms folded, when I finished talking. Som-kway
twisted a strand of her long white hair around her finger. Both watched me expectantly.

Som-kway glanced at Mah-kwa. "Which animal do
you think is the child's spirit animal?"

"I've never heard of anyone seeing so many visions
at one time! How extraordinary!" Mah-kwa said. "The
birds seem to like Mee-pahk. She saw a swan. However,
the old snapping turtle was the loudest voice. He has
been injured. He would be offended if we didn't pay
him special tribute."

Som-kway nodded. *"He, he!"* she exclaimed. *"Pam-boo-tes,* the snapping turtle, is the spirit guide. It is so."

"Yes. Besides, we are the Turtle people. It is a great honor that a turtle should talk to one of our young." Mah-kwa smiled widely, then burned some cedar leaves and dispersed the smoke with an eagle-wing fan. Brother and sister chanted a few prayers together.

"I would prefer to have the swan for my spirit guide," I said.

"Quiet, girl!" Som-kway scolded, then quickly returned to her chanting.

Over the next week Som-kway made me small clay figures of a turtle and swan to add to the medicine pouch they had given me at my adoption. Everything in the pouch had magical significance and would help me in my journey through life. Preparations for the *gam-wing* festival began, but I was still weak from my illness, so I stayed in the long house. I lost count of the days that I had been there. Finally I felt stronger and could eat solid food again. All but Som-kway and I moved out of the long house to stay in a special dwelling near a boulder called Mishow Rock on the southeastern part of the island. "The *gamwing* ceremony is important because it restores order to the universe," Som-kway said. "Mee-pahk, I would like you to sing and dance on the final day of the festivities."

I looked at Som-kway with horror. "Do you want me to talk about what I saw in front of the whole village?" I was on the verge of tears.

"Yes. Don't worry, my child. I will be with you."

Som-kway made me a new deerskin skirt and painted a big picture of a turtle on it.

"Mee-pahk, the boys in our village receive visions when they go off on their vision quests," she told me. "It is part of their passage to adulthood. But it is a rare and special thing for girls to receive visions. We talk about our spirit animals only to others on special occasions." She helped me to compose a little song about the turtle. I was to describe the turtle without specifically naming him.

"Stand up straight and proud," she said. "Move slowly. Enjoy each step."

● ● ●

When I entered the ceremonial house, it was large and dark and frightening. All the tribe sat around me. The room was heavy with tobacco and cedar smoke. The drummers began beating their skin drums. Somkway had me stand at the center of the circle. Everyone's gaze was fixed steadily upon me. Mah-kwa, dressed in the hideous red-and-black mask, passed a turtle-shell rattle to me. I was suddenly afraid and stepped back toward one of the doorways. I remembered the stories of my own mother, years before, standing in the courtroom in the little village of Roxbury, Massachusetts. "The Lord hath let me see which was the clear ministry and which the wrong. . . . I constantly receive revelations directly from God. I've never had any great thing done but that which was revealed to me beforehand."

"How do you know that it's God's word?" a member of the court asked.

"How did Abraham know that it was God who bade him offer his son?"

"By an immediate voice."

Mother replied, "So to me by an immediate revelation."

"Mrs. Hutchinson is unfit for our society, and she shall be banished out of our liberties and imprisoned till she be sent away."

A leper, they had said. An instrument of the devil. A babbling troublemaker. A Jezebel.

"Come here, child. Sing," Som-kway bade me now.

I looked all around at the gleaming, painted faces. There was Wam-pak. He had his usual expression— purposely blank, suppressed. I glanced at Sa-kat, surprised to find that she, like the others, had painted her face a fearsome red and yellow and had outlined her eyes in black. I stared at her for a moment. She held her back stiffly straight, as her father did. She was not Sa-kat but some demon! Was I still feverish?

"Sing," Som-kway said again. I sensed the growing excitement in the room. My throat felt dry.

Som-kway, hearty and smiling, took my hand with a new possessiveness. Her cheeks were flushed. She grasped the rattle, shook it, and began to sing. The others repeated the words of the song after her.

I stood rigid and looked at the faces of the people watching me. I felt a throbbing inside my head. My face grew very hot. I collapsed to the floor.

"The child is ill. Wam-pak, carry her back to the long house," I heard Som-kway say.

I felt too ill to protest, but Wam-pak lifted me gently.

That night the rain began to fall hard, and I tossed about feverishly. My mind went back to the time when my family had lived in Boston in the grand house with the fireplace that looked up to the sky. I was a very little girl then, plump and tall for my age. I loved the crowds that would come to hear my mother talk, big crowds of nearly a hundred women. Mother told them, "I will show you a way, if I can attain it, for you to have revelations of such ravishing joy that you should never have cause to be sorry for sin." The women would pick me up and tug at my red hair and give me gifts sometimes, a wooden top or perhaps a sugarplum.

My sisters had often told me the story of how, one warm autumn night, Mother preached to eighty women. Her eyes were animated, her hair parted under her tight cap. Governor Winthrop and the stern Reverend Cartwright stormed into the house.

Mother continued to speak on her favorite topic: It was the duty of every man and woman to follow the promptings of his or her inner voice, the Holy Spirit within. People did not need the intervention of the church. Then Mother aimed her next remark at the minister. "Going to heaven has nothing to do with the clergy."

"You are disrupting the peace! Break up this meeting immediately! Your talk is from the devil!" he said.

"I speak with the authority of God. I directly convey the words God speaks to me."

"I've never in my life heard such audacity!" Governor Winthrop said.

"How dare you challenge the voice of God within me!" Mother was almost enjoying herself.

"Leave or I will have you all arrested!" the governor said, and the women went scurrying.

"Wait!" Mother called, but not one of them stayed.

That was when Mother had been taken away as a prisoner of the colony.

"Mother! Mother!" I called out. Instead, Som-kway and Wam-pak sat over me. Wam-pak held a hunk of meat to his mouth.

Som-kway took me in her arms in as loving a way as my own mother ever had. I felt such relief to be with her.

I remembered the old snapping turtle and pictured him watching me with his narrow red eyes. I knew he was pleased with the amount of attention he had received.

The Silent Walker

ONCE THAT FALL, AFTER THE MEN WENT TO war, I woke up from a heavy sleep to hear a flapping of wings on the roof of the long house. It was the deepest part of the night. A nearly full moon shone through a smoke hole of the house and illuminated the world inside with gleaming gray light. I was aware of every detail in the room, the family around me a tangle of bodies, and the corn hanging from the ceiling. I turned to see that Som-kway was already sitting bolt upright on her sleeping platform.

Again there was a nervous fluttering sound.

"What is it, an owl?" I whispered.

"Shhh!" Som-kway hissed.

Som-kway's eyes were expectant, serious. I guessed the animal's visit must be a dreaded sign to her.

I clutched my medicine pouch, which I had started to keep near me when I slept.

The door of hanging skins burst open. An enormous bird with lustrous black feathers flew into the center of the room.

Suk-ee-loon-gawn screamed, and the baby began to cry. She held him closely.

Som-kway took a broom and swung for the bird. "Witch Woman, what do you want?" she shrieked.

The bird circled about the room in sweeping motions. Mee-kwun clapped his little hands in delight.

"Mee-pahk, draw the skins across the entranceway! A-*lup-see!*" Som-kway yelled at me, telling me to hurry.

But I was too late. The bird disappeared into the cool night air.

"What happened?" I asked.

"It was the witch, the Silent Walker," Som-kway said. "She's gone. She will not be bothering us anymore tonight."

In the morning Som-kway rose in a fury. She instructed Sa-kat and me to make model birds out of cornhusks to hang over Mee-kwun, Mee-mun-dut, and all the other young children in the village. She called the cornhusk figures "witch birds."

I had many questions, but no one seemed in a mood to talk.

Som-kway took some dried herbs from the ceiling and put them in a basket. She was in a great hurry to be off.

"Where are you going?" I asked Som-kway.

"To talk to the witch!" she answered. "You girls stay here."

When Som-kway had gone, I asked Sa-kat, "Was that a crow we saw last night?"

"I don't know," she said.

Suk-ee-loon-gawn answered. "It wasn't a crow. It was a *wing-gay-oh-kwet,* 'one who eats meat.' But it was really Noo-chee-kway, one of the Silent Walkers. She has taken souls from small bodies. She is evil."

I watched Sa-kat nervously fold the cornhusks into

wings. I tried to imitate her, though my birds were not nearly as delicate as hers.

"Why do you call these birds witch birds?" I asked Suk-ee-loon-gawn.

"Because they stand guard against the Silent Walkers," she said, giving me an impatient look. She thought me slow-witted for not understanding the signs of the villagers. She sighed, then went on. "Mee-mun-dut and Mee-kwun are still very young. The witch could suck out their souls. We must not let that happen."

I shivered and frowned. I watched as Sa-kat strung several birds together with sinew and hung them over Mee-mun-dut's cradle board.

Suk-ee-loon-gawn seemed to be burning with fever, and I did not want to go too close to her. After a while she took the baby to her breast.

Sa-kat and I made about a dozen witch birds, and then we decided to go find Som-kway. The air felt chilly, and the fog crept in from the water over the land. On such a day the canoes remained ashore and the villagers stayed at home to weave baskets, repair fishnets, string beads, or chip stones into the points that would tip arrows or spears. The surf pounded so loudly that at first I could not hear Som-kway shouting at Noo-chee-kway. The two stood on the beach, side by side, with Som-kway's stout form towering over the other. Witch Woman's stringy white hair blew into her face.

"Have you food in your storage pit?" Som-kway asked her.

"Yes," the woman answered.

"You will not live to see the end of your winter's supplies," Som-kway shouted.

Witch Woman turned toward Som-kway, hands on her hips. Her eyes shone in her weathered face. *"Ha! Ha!* So you think!"

"Come, children," Som-kway said, drawing us to her. Then she turned to Noo-chee-kway. "Don't you ever go flapping about in my house again or I'll cook you in a pot! I may cook you in a pot anyway!"

I had never seen Som-kway this angry!

Sa-kat and I followed her along the broken coast. The gulls flew low that day, and their cries sounded anxious. Both Sa-kat and Som-kway looked about cautiously, as if we were being watched.

A vague terror filled me. What if Noo-chee-kway was innocent, like my own mother or her friend Mary Dyer, who people thought were witches? In the Massachusetts Bay Colony, any woman who said she'd had visions was considered a witch.

"How do you know Noo-chee-kway is a witch?" I asked Som-kway.

"I have seen her off in the woods with her ceremonies. Witches have their ceremonies alone. We have ours together. Also, witches—the Silent Walkers—have bad medicine. That means they use their power to cause illness, not healing."

"Do you think she will harm us?"

"Perhaps, but there's nothing to worry about at this moment, Mee-pahk," Som-kway told me. "The Silent Walkers have no power during the day. It is only at night that they have power."

"Are you going to kill her?" I asked.

Som-kway reflected. "Yes, perhaps, or someone else in the village will kill her. As I said, she will die before her storage pit is empty."

"I don't understand! What has she done?"

"She has a witch's bundle. I've seen it," Som-kway answered in her low, gruff voice. "About once a year, the bundle cries out, *'Hum-mee! Hum-mee!* Feed me!' She must feed it human blood, or else it will take revenge on her and terrible things will happen to her and her entire family."

I remembered tales of old hags who made pacts with the devil and flew through the sky on broomsticks. They were brought to trial, stripped naked, and searched for the devil's marks. Mother had said these women were falsely accused by their enemies. After the women were hanged, their rivals claimed their belongings.

If I'd still been living in Boston, I myself could be hanged for witchcraft!

Oh, please, Som-kway, I prayed silently, *do not kill her. Mother in heaven! Please, God. Keep us all safe from this witch, if she truly is a witch.*

I did not know if Som-kway was right. Still, I was on her side. I helped to gather the plants and prepare them. The fog seemed to part for Som-kway as she walked so that she could find what she was looking for in the woods. "We are lucky," she said. "The first frost is a very good time to gather plants. Our spirit guides will help us to defeat this witch."

The Doll Being

Som-kway used the plants she had gathered to fortify Place of Stringing Beads village against evil spirits. She ignited red cedar branches, then hung clumps of dried mullein leaves over entranceways.

During the next few days, as we sheltered ourselves from a cold, gray rain that shook the leaves from the trees, Som-kway made me a doll out of soft hide. I thought this was strange, but I loved dolls. Kate and I had had many dolls made of rags and cornhusks.

My new doll had only slits for eyes, and I couldn't help being disappointed by this. She had a straight nose, and she wore a deerskin shawl with dyed-porcupine-quill designs, deerskin leggings, a shell necklace, and little beaded moccasins. Som-kway used some of Sa-kat's hair for her head.

"Thank you," I said to Som-kway. I named her Kate, even though she was distinctly Lenape in appearance. Holding Kate gave me a comfort I had not known in a very long time. My pleasure soon turned to horror when Som-kway said, "That is an *oh-tas*. It is not an ordinary doll. I have given it a spirit. Your doll is alive!"

. . .

"Soon it will be time to dance the dolls," Sa-kat explained when we were alone in the long house one day.

"I don't understand," I said.

"Dolls need to be danced and fed in order to guard the health of the family," she said.

I held Kate close to me.

Sa-kat went on. "Som-kway made the doll being to protect you from the witch." Sa-kat took out a large basket hidden far in back of one of the sleeping platforms. She carefully opened the lid. "I promised Som-kway I wouldn't show these to you until you had learned our ways. Now you have. Look!" she said. The slitted eyes of about a dozen dolls peered out at us. Sa-kat was even more frightened than I was.

"They're beautiful," I said, taking one out. It was a boy *oh-tas* with an elaborate beaded headband.

"I've seen one breathe," Sa-kat whispered.

I studied the dolls, all motionless, and shivered. My face tightened in anticipation. I almost believed her.

Sa-kat threw back her hair. Her eyes looked wild. She took out the dolls one by one and inspected the bottoms of their little moccasins.

"The dolls move about during the night," she said. "Look!"

Sure enough, the little moccasins had bits of fresh green moss on them.

The Lenape believed that even good powers were likely to turn evil if they were not given gifts. All spirits and doll beings must be fed, or else the owner would come to grief. I was the only one in the village who felt that the world did not act in that way. Yet I had forgotten much of my mother's religion. Now I too wanted to please the Great Spirit.

Wam-pak and the warriors asked Som-kway to look at the signs in the sky to forecast the weather for the next few days. When it was time for the dolls to be danced, Som-kway selected a clearing in the woods, and logs were placed in a square for seating. Wam-pak and two helpers brought back a large buck, which was then prepared and cooked. Som-kway and Mah-kwa fastened all the dolls on poles. "Give me your doll being," Som-kway said. Reluctantly I let Kate be taken away from me to be paraded around with the other dolls.

Som-kway used the ceremonial eagle-feather fan to blow cedar smoke up to the heavens. Then she held my doll on its pole and chanted softly to it.

"What's she saying?" I asked Sa-kat.

"She's calling the doll being *noo-huma,* 'grandmother,' and telling it that we are about to have a dance in its honor. She is asking it to please grant good health to you and all our family."

The drummers sitting at the center of the dance ground began to beat furiously on their skin drums. Som-kway, holding the doll being in front of her, began to dance around the drummers, hopping a bit, then turning and twisting while singing a mournful song. The rest of the villagers followed, forming a snakelike line.

"Now we join them!" Sa-kat said.

I hopped and sang with the others, moving to the drumbeat. I coughed from the heavy cedar smoke. For a moment I felt dizzy and short of breath. Then something turned in the air. I could breathe more easily. My voice gathered in the raw bottom of my throat. I sang out, deep and strong, and joined the rising tide of the chant.

There were many dolls to be danced and songs to be sung. After a round of about six or seven dolls, everyone rested.

When it was time to feed the dolls, Som-kway unfastened Kate and handed her to me. I watched as the others all "fed" their dolls, holding food to their frozen, painted lips, then eating the food themselves.

As I pretended to feed Kate, I ate the sweet venison and drank the cool spring water. What would Mother and my sisters think of the doll dance?

When all had fallen silent and the torches were lit, a large full moon rose in the sky. A child called out, "Where is Mee-kwun?"

Suk-ee-loon-gawn shrieked. "My baby!" One moment we had all seen him playing with the little children, chewing on deer fat, and another moment he was nowhere to be found.

"It's the witch!" Som-kway cried out. "Has anyone seen her?"

No one had.

Som-kway had appointed Chah-kol and Tu-ma to watch Noo-chee-kway's wigwam, but she had sneaked out sometime during the festivities.

For hours we looked frantically for Mee-kwun. "Mee-kwun! Boy!" we called. We broke into search parties and went to the village, to the springs, to the beaches. Sa-kat and I joined Chah-kol and Tu-ma and some of the older boys. Finally Tu-ma suggested, "We should go off the island to the burial ground. This is where we will likely find the witch."

We took two of the largest canoes, pushing our way through the darkness. The water was choppy and the paddling was hard.

We left the canoes on the beach and followed one of the hunters' paths through the forest. The trees filled with wind, and their massive old trunks creaked. These were the trees with the most life force, and capable of the greatest conversations.

In the burial ground we wandered among the grave markers. I thought of Suk-ah-sun, buried in his crouching position with his tools and weapons beside him.

"The witch could be in any form . . . a bird, perhaps, or a dog," Sa-kat said.

I imagined the souls of the dead everywhere, floating through the trees, drifting back to the village and passing through the walls of the wigwams.

I was frightened not by the shadows but by the terrible final memory of my little brother, Zuriel. He had been the same age as Mee-kwun, just the age to be an angel and a pest. I didn't want anything to happen to Mee-kwun!

I looked up. A big dog stood in the middle of the burial ground, staring out at us. Its coat was streaked with dust and glistened in the moonlight.

"It is the Silent Walker, in the form of a dog-wolf," Chah-kol said. "Everyone, surround her!"

She paced about nervously. I had never seen such a large dog.

Chah-kol stood about a foot away from the dog. He stretched the heavy blade of a tomahawk above his head and swung, aiming for the skull. Instead he struck her on the side of her neck and on her front right paw. The dog yelped in pain.

The boys threw stones, and one hit the dog on the head, but the blow was not hard enough to kill. Snarling, she leaped and locked her teeth onto Chah-kol's hand. Tu-ma pounced on her. The dog let go, ran into the woods, and seemed to vanish into thin air.

"Chah-kol! Are you all right?" I asked.

"Noo-la-mul-see," he said, "I am well." He stood up. His hand was bleeding.

"We almost had her!" Tu-ma said. "If one of us had only struck her right, she would be dead."

"You're all torn up, Chah-kol," Sa-kat said. "We should go home. Wam-pak will find the witch."

We walked along the paths to the shore, the moon high overhead. Sa-kat whispered to me, "You have had visions, Mee-pahk. Try to have a vision now. Ask your spirit animals to find Mee-kwun."

I drew back. I wasn't at all sure of my talents, as Mother had been. "I don't think I can have visions by trying to make them happen," I said.

"Try," she said.

"No, it wouldn't be right."

Sa-kat held my arm. "If you have a talent for visions, you must use it," she said. "Hurry! The Silent Walker will gain her greatest power soon, in the middle of the night."

How could I explain that I was the daughter of a woman whose visions had been her downfall? I thought again about how many people considered my mother trouble. And I, trouble's daughter, was becoming like her.

Besides, sometimes Mother had made mistakes. Hadn't Mother said that God would deliver her from any calamity? Pushing this idea from my mind, I prayed to God and to the Great Spirit for Mee-kwun's safety.

I closed my eyes and tried to form a picture of Mee-kwun hiding somewhere, but nothing came. For a fleeting moment I saw the snapping turtle, his little flat head in profile, his large lower jaw tucked under. This time the talkative turtle said nothing. He seemed content. Then I pictured an owl coming out of my forehead. The owl had a white, heart-shaped face. She flew high up into a tall pine on Place of Stringing Beads island and stared out of a little round hole where a branch had once been.

"I see an owl high up in a tree. The tree is on the island, near the pine groves. . . . I have a feeling that Mee-kwun is back there somewhere. I don't think he's here."

We went back to Place of Stringing Beads island, to the pine groves where all the *kook-hoos-uk*, the owls, lived.

I recalled the tall tree I had seen in my mind and went to it.

The Healing

"MEE-KWUN!" I CALLED.

Mee-kwun waddled out from behind the tree. He was bundled up in furs and his dark eyes stared out from his little face, framed with a raccoon tail. Everyone yelled and rushed toward him. He laughed.

"Where have you been? We've been so worried about you!" I said.

"Dog. Big dog." His eyes were dark and blank. He did not even recognize us.

We took Mee-kwun back to the village, where Suk-ee-loon-gawn, Wam-pak, and the others welcomed him with many caresses and little pecks on his face. I felt hurt. Everyone was so excited to see him that they did not bother to greet me.

Then Som-kway said, "You have done well, my children. I am proud of you. But Mee-kwun is still in great danger. His soul is missing. We must have the ceremony before more time passes."

Som-kway ordered Sa-kat to find Mah-kwa and asked me to build up the fires in the long house. Suk-ee-loon-gawn laid Mee-kwun on a bundle of skins. By the time Mah-kwa appeared, Som-kway had already smoked a pipeful of tobacco and was sitting upright near the fire in a trance. She moaned in a low voice, asking the spirit helpers to join her. Mah-kwa sat down and chanted along with his sister. Mah-kwa's family—his wife, Kee-kee-cheem-wes, and his sons, Chah-kol and Tu-ma—also came into our long house to watch.

"Som-kway is going to the spirit world to bring back Mee-kwun's soul," Sa-kat whispered. "Only medicine people know the way."

After a time Som-kway opened her eyes. "Fetch me a bowl," she ordered Sa-kat. What happened next was very strange. Som-kway made motions with her hands to transfer something invisible, something quite heavy—Mee-kwun's soul—into the bowl. Then, while Mee-kwun sat upright in Suk-ee-loon-gawn's lap, Som-kway gently poured the soul into the little boy through the top of his head.

Mee-kwun suddenly jolted as if he had been slapped on the back. His eyes returned to their usual mischievous expression. Then he started to cry. Suk-ee-loon-gawn held him tightly while she offered me a grateful look.

We had a small feast, followed by some dancing. The night faded away. Weary and exhausted, my Lenape family slept in our long house with Mah-kwa's family and a few others, their arms and legs overlapping. I could not sleep. I felt proud of myself for my vision; it had helped people. But I kept thinking of Mother and the people who said she was in league with the devil-snake. I had experienced my own power. I liked it and didn't like it, at the same time.

The next day Sa-kat and I followed Som-kway to the witch's wigwam. She had a terrible cut on her neck, in the exact place where Chah-kol had struck the dog with the hand axe. Two fingers were missing from the witch's right hand.

To make a salve for wounds, Som-kway usually made a mixture of black-walnut bark, pounded into powder and mixed with grease. But today she did not offer to help Noo-chee-kway. The witch woman lay on her sleeping platform, moaning, her small rodentlike face contorted in pain and her tangled hair spread about her.

This woman truly is *a witch,* I thought. Was there some way Som-kway could make her stop doing evil things without killing her?

"Where is the bundle?" Som-kway demanded.

Noo-chee-kway turned toward the wall.

Som-kway told us that the evil bundle must be somewhere nearby. We would know it because, hungry for the taste of blood, it would be whispering, *"Hum-mee! Hum-mee!* Feed me! Feed me!"

But we did not find the bundle. Som-kway left the witch alone in her house. Soon after, Noo-chee-kway disappeared. Som-kway surmised that the witch had chosen to die in animal form, off in the woods somewhere. Or perhaps she'd been killed in animal form. It was lucky that we had not heard a howling wolf-dog, for surely that would have been a harbinger of doom. As for the bundle, she hoped the witch had buried it so that it would stop bringing trouble to our village. The world had righted itself again, at least for a time.

Wam-pak led the young men of the village off to war. The villagers left behind were not interested in their usual pleasures. They ate their stews and corn bread in silence. The air grew chilly, and even the children began to spend more time indoors. The smoke of indoor cooking fires filled the wigwams and long houses.

On one such gray autumn night my Lenape family cooked on the beach. The boys of the village had netted what was probably the season's last catch of flounder and stripers in the lagoon. There was a horde of gulls watching us eagerly. They stood in rows along the beach. The water seemed unusually still, as if it might rain later on.

It was during that odd, quiet, cold evening that Suk-ee-loon-gawn seemed an entirely different person to me. Her broad face was very beautiful, I thought, in the way that people who are brave or kind are beautiful. I had not seen this in her before. The corners of her mouth did not turn down that night. She did not treat me with her usual tolerant scorn; her heart was a little more open to me. As she sat on skins with her baby on her lap and Mee-kwun, Sa-kat, and I all crowded around her, she sang sad songs that had words I did not understand. We were all Suk-ee-loon-gawn's children. It seemed that her love for us all was utter and equal.

"You brought back Mee-kwun, my little feather," she whispered to me. Then, with her baby in her arms, she rocked. She put her hand on my shoulder and rocked me at the same time, singing in a thin voice. Mother had had her own rocking motion. Each had her own distinct way.

Suddenly a thought came to me. Suk-ee-loon-gawn was usually sharp in the tongue. That was her trademark. She insulted people and was very sure of herself. Whom else had I ever met with a sharp tongue but my own mother! Perhaps Suk-ee-loon-gawn was more like my mother than I had thought. She was intelligent, she was contrary, she was single-minded. Like Mother, she had a desperate urge to be noticed; Suk-ee-loon-gawn was vain, wearing more jewelry and finery than any other woman in the village, and she liked to shout. She nursed grudges. Perhaps I was this way, too. Like me, the hurts of the world clung to her. It was a pleasant shock to meet a kindred spirit in the place where I had least expected it.

Suk-ee-loon-gawn's children and I sat in the hum of her voice and let the feeling of stillness and peace wash over us. For that moment we were united. We seemed to share in the knowledge that terrible things had happened to both of us.

"*Nee-chan,*" Suk-ee-loon-gawn called me as she rocked me. "My daughter."

Awakening

QUITE UNEXPECTEDLY, I BEGAN MY TRAINING as a medicine woman under Som-kway that winter. "It is much colder on the other side of the island. I noticed when I was walking," I said to her one morning.

Som-kway was looking at the water, as she often did. I didn't think I had said anything important, but a flash of excitement lit up in her dark eyes. She smiled at me with her full, cracked lips. *"Yoo-ho!"* she shrieked, and slapped her thigh. "There is hope for you, little Mee-pahk. Maybe one of these days you will wake up and come out of your daze."

Daze? Was I living my life in a perpetual daze? Whenever I fell into thoughts about my mother and the family, I didn't notice the world around me.

"Now, Mee-pahk, can you tell me *why* it is colder on the other side of the island?"

Under her serious gaze, I was afraid to guess. *"Tak-ta-nee*—I don't know."

"Where does the sun rise?" She was growing impatient.

"The sun rises in the east and sets in the west," I said, relieved. For once I knew the answer.

"*Yooh!*" As always, there was a hard uprightness in her deep voice. "We receive the most warmth and sunlight on this side of our island because we are in the southeast. Now I have another question for you. In what direction is the wind blowing?"

"I don't know."

"I will teach you one way to tell," she said. "Look at the gulls. Gulls always face into the wind. See, they are turning a little as the wind is changing direction. The wind is coming from the northeast."

"You are wise," I said. My words set her into a fit of laughter. Her great weight expanded her straining skirt as she laughed.

I remembered instances when she had pointed out certain things to me: the storm ring around a bright moon or the shapes of the clouds hidden in a white sky. Many times there was a spacious silence between us. That silence was part of the teaching, too.

"You are my teacher," I said.

"And you have a lot to learn," Som-kway replied.

Som-kway returned to mixing her remedies, ending the conversation. But there was one more thing I needed to find out. "Are you teaching me to be a medicine woman?"

"Yes, perhaps, if the spirits, the *ma-nu-too-wuk,* desire it and if you remain pure of heart. Now why don't you make yourself useful and fetch us some firewood?"

Som-kway's response filled me with joy. At that moment I wanted nothing else but to become a wise woman like her. There was an element of mystery in the idea that renewed something in me. How wonderful to be able to interpret visions and to make medicines that could cure people. Was I becoming a person who would

114

have pleased Mother? But still, I was afraid to be different from everyone else. Like my mother, I was marked for life.

Sa-kat was Som-kway's other apprentice, and each of us had our own talents. Sa-kat understood far more of herbs, medicines, and chants than I ever would. She had a better memory than I and was more observant. But I was the only girl in the community who'd had visions.

The snow fell steadily for days. It clung deeply to the trees in the woods and fell in heavy masses on the wigwams and long houses of our village. We wore leggings and cloaks and used our snowshoes to move about. Once more the lagoon separating Place of Stringing Beads island from Two Island froze over, and the ducks spread out like hundreds of dirty specks on the ice.

We stocked the long house with enough wood to last for the winter, my second one with the Lenape. Wam-pak and the young men brought back deer for us to eat. This time Tu-ma, Chah-kol, and the other boys my age joined in the hunting parties. The boys stayed in our village, however, when it was time for the men to go to battle. Tu-ma and Chah-kol resented being left behind, and after days of being cooped up inside, every one of us in the village became cross and out of sorts. The long house felt crowded; it smelled horribly of body odors, greasy skins, and wet furs. Mee-mun-dut cried at night, and Suk-ee-loon-gawn did not seem in a hurry to replace the mosses between his little legs, even when the whole house stank from him. The ditch behind the long house that served as a privy also smelled rank.

I grew impatient for change.

"It's cold. It has been snowing too much," I said.

"What is life offering you now?" Som-kway said. "If it is cold, we accept that. If it is hot, we accept that also. All things change. Even the most perfect things change. No matter how terrible your surroundings are, you can learn to find peace. In the stillness, what is beautiful will reveal itself."

I did not understand, but I did not argue with her.

"Mee-pahk, I know that life has offered you much pain," Som-kway continued. "Remember this: The waves come crashing down on the shore. But we can learn to maneuver these waves a bit while we are in our canoes."

Another day, when Som-kway was showing me how to slice venison into narrow strips, she said, "You have a little cleft on the tip of your nose. It was one of the first things I noticed about you."

"What of it?" I said angrily. I was tired of work and being indoors.

"It is the cleft that shows you have a division in your heart."

"I don't understand."

"You live in two worlds, here with the Lenape, and there with your own people. You will always be divided."

So Som-kway truly understood me. As usual with her, a casual remark could lead to some ominous message. I especially disliked the times Som-kway foretold the future. This frightened me.

"What about the cleft on my nose? You think it's a bad sign, don't you?" I pressed.

"*Koo!*" she said. "No. These indicators are neither

good nor bad. Your nose is just part of who you are. After a while we learn to love our faces."

My father had had a cleft on his nose also. Did he too have a divided heart? I remembered that he always missed England.

"What else do you see in my face?" I asked.

Som-kway reflected for a moment as she hung the strips of meat on long poles of hickory wood. She kept the flames down low by sprinkling the fire with a little water, creating smoke that billowed into my eyes.

"I see that your eyebrows are growing long and full. When you first came to us, there was a little break in one—when you almost died with your family. Now the break has grown in and you have moved past it."

"You can tell the future. Will I ever return to my own people?" I asked.

"That I don't know."

"Som-kway, I have brothers and sisters who are still living. They live far away. Deep in my heart I have always felt I would find them someday."

"*Nooh-wee-tee,* my grandchild, you are growing strong; you will find out what you are supposed to do in your life. But do not be impatient! Everything is not revealed to us at once. Perhaps it is the will of the Great Spirit that you should live your life here. Or it may be that you leave us. Sometimes in life we must make difficult choices. We do one thing or another. There is sadness because we cannot do both things, be in two places at once. I see that your path is difficult, Mee-pahk, because of this divided heart. For now, try not to worry. Everything in its time. I will tell you all that I know: You will have a long and full life. It is I who will die soon."

I stared at her. "What makes you think so?"

"I feel it in my bones. It's something I know."

"When?"

"Not this winter, not for at least another year. I've looked for signs in the sky and haven't seen anything to indicate otherwise."

"I don't want to hear you say you're going to die!" I said. "My brother-in-law Will used to say that it is dangerous to pay too much attention to signs and portents. He said that it caused much trouble for Mother."

"If we pay more attention to signs and portents than everything else that is going on all around us, then we have gotten ourselves off the clear path of true understanding. At the same time, *nooh-wee-tee*, you must learn not to be afraid to see indicators of what will come. Now find the others. It is time to eat some of this good meat!"

I was worried, both for Som-kway and for myself. That night I dreamed of a rabbit, half brown and wild, and half pure white, like a pet rabbit I had seen in Boston when I was a small child. In my dream I also met the snapping turtle once again. He was still grumbling, but he seemed happy enough.

Pleased with my dream, Som-kway painted pictures of rabbits and turtles on small stones for me to add to my medicine pouch. She told me a story of how, in the beginning of time, all the world rested on the back of a turtle.

"One day Kee-shay-lu-moo-kawng, Our Creator Who Created Us by His Thoughts, was lonely. The world was nothing but water, and he wanted company. So he made a great turtle that swam the ocean. The turtle rose from the water, and out of the mud on its back a cedar tree grew. A sprout on the turtle's back became the first man. The tree bent over and touched the ground. From this place the first woman emerged. The man and the woman became the original parents for all the people in the world."

The story was not unlike the tale of Adam and Eve. I believed Mother would have liked it. How I missed reading the Bible with Kate and Annie and Mother!

"You see now how important turtles are to our people," Som-kway explained. "It is good that you have a turtle for your spirit guide. He will give you strength when I die. You will need strength. There will be troubled times ahead in our village."

"Troubled times?"

But Som-kway would say no more.

The Visitor

IN THE WEEKS FOLLOWING, I THOUGHT OF the rabbit of two colors. *I must not forget my old ways,* I told myself. If I ever found a way to be with my family, I would be ready for them.

One day I attempted to show Sa-kat how to read and write with a goose-quill pen and oak gall ink that I had made.

"What are you doing?" Sa-kat asked. Sa-kat, Som-kway, and Suk-ee-loon-gawn all stared at me suspiciously.

"I'm writing. Look here. This is English. I'm making the alphabet. *A, B, C, D* . . ." I handed the quill to Sa-kat. "Now you try."

I could not interest her in this pursuit for more than a few minutes. She did not understand the concept of an alphabet.

"To learn our ABCs, we used to make up rhymes, like this," I said. " '*A*, in Adam's fall we sinned all,' or '*D*, a dog will bite a thief at night.' "

My Indian family just looked at me in puzzlement. Even Som-kway, who was interested in all the things of the world, was not responding to me. In the end I gave up. I couldn't translate the rhymes very well, and it was too cold to do much writing. The ink soon froze. Instead, Sa-kat and I rubbed red stones together with spit and painted each other's faces. We got along best when Sa-kat showed me how to do things her way. Still, I yearned to teach her something of the world from which I had come.

"Sewing with these porcupine quills is a lot like what my people would call embroidery," I told her. "We'd make a little sampler with cross-stitches. In time, working in the dim firelight, a girl could almost make herself blind from sewing so much."

"*Ha!* Those foolish white girls. They make themselves blind!" Sa-kat jeered.

"English girls don't rub smelly animal grease all over their bodies!"

"*Cheet-kwu-see!* Now that you speak our language, all you do is talk!" Sa-kat said.

"It's true," Suk-ee-loon-gawn piped up. Though she liked me better now, she continued to insult me. "That salt person, she talks too much!"

Mee-kwun was the only one who could suspend judgment long enough to listen to me. He sucked his fingers, staring incredulously at me as I talked. I said to Mee-kwun—and to all the others, who I was sure were listening—that in the colonies there were beautiful bridges made of stone to take people across rivers.

My people wore high-collared shirts, I said, instead of running about naked. On Sundays dancing was not allowed. Swimming was against the law. Laughing was against the law on the Lord's Day. But sometimes people overlooked all those rules.

Suk-ee-loon-gawn and Som-kway glanced at each

other with their eyebrows raised. "No dancing? No swimming? No laughing?"

"Yes," I answered. Was that so terrible?

"These white people make a cold, stern effort to do good," Suk-ee-loon-gawn said. "They fail. Then they cannot face themselves. These people must have a lot of pride!"

"Pride is not an excuse not to do what is right," Som-kway added.

"They are not *bad* people," I said. In confusion I turned away from the women and met Sa-kat's gaze. She eyed me tenderly.

"Everything with you is good or evil, Mee-pahk. These sharp divisions need to melt," Som-kway added, though not unkindly.

A sudden rage welled up in me. Good or evil! "Wam-pak and the warriors should not have killed my family!" I said angrily.

A chill swept across the room. Everyone was respectfully silent in deference to the dead.

"I am sorry for what happened," Som-kway said. "But my people are at war with your people."

"Do you think Wam-pak was right in killing my mother?" I said. My fist was clenched.

Som-kway sighed, then said, "My daughter's husband is a warrior chief. Our elders decided that our young men would go to war. It is our way to avenge our enemies."

"The Dutch are your enemies. We were an English family living on Dutch land," I said, tears welling up.

"The land was the land of my people. It was not Dutch land," she said.

"Wam-pak should not have killed my mother."

"Some of your people were killed, and many more of our people were slaughtered. I am sorry that your mother, brothers, and sisters had to die. This is what happens in war," she said.

I trembled and shook. Then I exploded in a fit of crying. "I wish I had never come here!"

"Killing is never right," Som-kway said, without taking her eyes away from me. "Killing leads to more killing. I don't like it when Wam-pak and the other warriors go off to battle. But what happened could not have been avoided, my child. What has happened in the past is now bearing fruit in the present. It is a giant wave that has not yet crashed. It is a pattern working itself out."

"But Wam-pak had a choice! He chose to kill my family. He wanted them to die!"

Som-kway sighed. She rested her hands on my trembling shoulders. "Wam-pak is a warrior. Wam-pak fights to protect his people from harm. He did not start the war. But there is something else I wish to tell you, Mee-pahk. Peace *is* possible. We can avoid future conflicts by the way we act. We must do the best we can and dedicate our actions to the spirits. Ignorance is destroyed only by awakening to knowledge. Peace can occur between people when there is understanding. . . . But I know that you are too young to follow all I am saying. There is not much I can say to comfort you. I'm sorry that your mother and brothers and sisters are dead, Mee-pahk. We share your sorrow because we have felt the same pain."

This was the closest to an apology that I would ever get. I knew it, but it was not enough. I could no longer hear Som-kway's words.

I thought of Suk-ee-loon-gawn's lost daughter. I looked about me at the women and children, layered in many different pieces of clothing. All their hands were rough and sore from the cold. They looked worn out. These people had been kind to me; they shared everything they had with me. Even Wam-pak . . . in his way, he had protected me.

The next day Sa-kat gave me a gift of some dyed porcupine quills and helped me sew pretty designs on my clothing. She tried so hard to help me to be happy. I could no longer hate the Lenape, even when I wanted to.

The wind stirred, making whirlwinds in the snow. There came a blizzard of remarkable ferocity that night, and the water, rising up with a terrible roar, destroyed the huts closest to the beach. My face and hands ached from the cold. Som-kway boiled hot drinks, but it seemed that nothing would drive the chill out of me.

Som-kway gradually trusted me enough to go with her and Sa-kat as she healed people in the village. When someone had a sprain or a broken bone, she was clever at fashioning a splint out of rawhide. We cured earaches by putting raccoon grease into people's ears. We treated burns with a salve made from powdered cattails ground with animal fat. I found I liked this sort of work.

By the time the ice broke in the early spring, the warriors had returned. There were several Lenape men from a different band with them. But the Dutch had killed nine more of our warriors. Again the women of the village smeared soot onto their faces. Some cut their hair. They looked like ghosts.

Back in the village I watched Wam-pak unpack his

sack. Among his things were an iron axe, a hoe, and a red blanket. I froze, remembering my own family's deaths. I cried out helplessly. Som-kway came and stood a little nearer to me.

But this time I joined in as the women wailed for their dead husbands. It felt good to cry out. Suk-ee-loon-gawn and I shrieked the loudest of everyone.

Halfway across the clearing Wam-pak raised his brows ever so slightly and gave me a look that meant he was happy to see me again. How could he feel this way after murdering another family of white people?

"Why didn't Wam-pak kill me?" I asked Som-kway later.

"In you he saw his own daughter. He liked you."

"How could he like me? I was the enemy."

"He liked your red hair and your serious little face. He thought you would make a good companion for Sa-kat. Wam-pak still likes you—can't you see that?"

The men began to assemble for a dance. It was then that I noticed one of the visiting warriors had lighter skin. He was a grown man, about Wam-pak's age. If the man's hair had not been shaved, it would have been light brown or even blond.

"Who are these warriors?" I asked Sa-kat.

"They're Wappingers," she replied. "They joined our warriors for a battle. They are resting here for a few days before returning to their own people."

"That man looks different from the rest," I said.

"I don't recognize him," Sa-kat replied.

The Wappingers circled with our own warriors to the fast drumbeat of a victory dance. I watched the fair-skinned man. He was observing me as well. Though he knew the warriors' dances, something about this man did not seem right. His blue eyes were narrow and unfocused. From time to time he cried out shrilly, as if he were wounded.

When our eyes met, I drew back in terror. Sparks of anger came from him.

The Agreement

THE STRANGE MAN TOOK ME ASIDE. HE GRABBED my wrist, looking about to make sure no one was listening. His hold was too tight. His long, dirty fingernails dug into my skin.

"Who are you?" he demanded in Lenape. His expression looked wild. "Are you an Indian captive? Are you for the Indians or are you against them?"

"Who are *you*?" I asked. I released myself from his grip.

"My name is Pieter Van Hook. I am Dutch. I am a trader," the man said, "though I travel with the Wappingers." The trader then tried to speak Dutch. I shook my head. Then we spoke in Lenape.

"I'm English. My name is Susanna Hutchinson. M-My other name is Mee-pahk," I stammered.

The trader reached out to touch my hair. "You're not Dutch?" I stepped back, startled. I did not like the way he studied me, red-eyed. Wrapped tightly in his Lenape cloak, he hunched forward. He began to mutter. What was wrong with him? "Have the Indians tortured you?"

"No!" I replied. "No!"

"Are you happy living with them?"

I was so startled by the question that I remained silent.

"You're lonely for your mother, aren't you?"

"Yes," I said. How had he read my mind?

The man's voice drained suddenly to less than a whisper as he said, "The Wappingers took my wife captive two years ago. My daughter was taken by another tribe. I go from place to place looking for them. For a moment I thought you were my child."

His expression softened when he spoke of his daughter. I felt sorry he had lost his wife and little girl.

I related my story, feeling guilty that I was betraying my Lenape family. But how good it felt to be talking to this man! I sensed he understood my troubles. The Dutchman swayed back and forth unsteadily as I talked. A fly settled on his face. It didn't seem to bother him.

"Do you have any living relations in the colonies?" he asked.

"Yes," I answered. "I have brothers and sisters in Narragansett and in Boston."

"Would they pay to have you ransomed?"

"Yes, I'm sure they would."

My heart pounded with hope. I imagined my brothers and sisters thought I was dead. For all I knew, they themselves could be dead of some epidemic—or returned to England.

"Would you like me to arrange it?" the man asked.

"Yes." I stopped breathing. I felt my face go white. The news seemed almost too good to be true.

I told him all I could remember about my brothers and sisters. Yes, they were all wealthy; they owned much land in both Narragansett and the Massachusetts Bay

Colony. My brother Edward and his wife, Catherine, had stayed in Boston to care for the house there, since my parents feared it would be seized after Mother's banishment. Father had been a textile merchant, and so my family also had farmland outside town with many cows and sheep. . . . As I remembered these details, I felt more and more hope.

His hand trembled as he spoke. The poor man had seen much tragedy.

"When I leave here, I will go with the Wappingers, your Lenape neighbors," Pieter Van Hook said, "but before long I will find a way back to the fort in New Amsterdam."

He did not say much more to me that night, except that the Dutch appeared to be winning the war, though both sides suffered heavy losses. The Indians outnumbered the white men. The Dutch had a very small army—resources were scarce—but recently they had hired a British general named John Underhill, who had annihilated the Pequots in the Massachusetts Bay Colony. Hope was in sight for the Dutch, he said, and for a captive like me, especially for a child of a wealthy English family.

But why hadn't they come for me already? Would a ransom truly be so easy to arrange?

Two days later, in a rainy mist, Pieter Van Hook left with his Wappinger companions. We had not spoken again.

• • •

I waited expectantly throughout the rainy winter months. Oh, the joy of returning to my family! By now I'd have many nieces and nephews.

But when the time came, how would I tell Sa-kat and Som-kway that I was leaving? Every time I looked into their faces, I recalled that I had not told them about the Dutchman. How could I hurt Sa-kat? I tried to push the thought away and picture how wonderful it would be to see my sisters Faith and Bridget again.

But was the trader a man to be trusted? What was it that made me feel good about Pieter Van Hook? What was it that made me feel bad? I remembered the way he had stood ankle deep in leaves, humming to himself, then muttering occasionally. I remembered the sad way he had looked when he told me about his daughter. The conversation had occurred so quickly. I hadn't the vaguest notion of what he would do next. Would he truly write to my family? What if the ransom wasn't successful? If I ran away and then was returned to the Lenape, they would kill me this time.

My old turtle looked at me suspiciously in a dream. He warned me not to be too confident. It was better to hide in one's shell; then there would be less risk for disappointment. "Turtle," I said, holding him and rubbing a salve into his cut, "you will be fine. No one is going to hurt you. Now that I have found you, I will never let you go."

• • •

Spring came, and once again, while the trees remained brown and leafless, the marsh grass grew rich, brilliant, and green, a thick grassy border around our island. There was the feeling of change, of activities and decisions being made, of the men returning from hunting and warfare, of fishing the river and inlets, of readying the fields for planting.

One day I stood on the beach near the mounds and mounds of empty clam and mussel shells. I noticed that the waves of the surf broke in different places each time. I watched the gulls turn their heads into the wind, and I thought of Som-kway, who was always eager for me to live life with greater attention. "Walk slowly, deeply, enjoy each step. Breathe through your feet," she told me.

How I would miss Place of Stringing Beads village!

Well, any number of things could happen to prevent the Dutchman from reaching my family. But no, he would succeed. I remembered the way he had clutched my arm.

I tried to pretend to Som-kway that nothing had changed. Her sharp mind knew better. "Once again your mind is cluttered and confused. Tell me what has happened."

But I could not answer her.

The Egg and Its Shell

THAT SPRING SOM-KWAY TOOK SA-KAT AND me in her canoe. In low marshy places between the island and the path on the shore, Som-kway pointed out some of the medicinal plants she used.

"We never take the first plant of its kind that we see," Som-kway said. When Som-kway removed a plant, she threw a pinch of tobacco into the hole that she left behind and quickly covered it. This was done as an offering of thanks. Each plant was given its own chant, which Som-kway had me practice.

"What are these chants for?" I asked. I was tired of learning them.

"For the plant, and also for the people we are healing," she said.

I repeated a long chant but stopped somewhere in the middle, the words forgotten. "I still don't see why I have to do this," I grumbled.

Memorizing did not come easily to me. Besides, I thought, I would be rescued any day now.

"If you say the chant wrong, you might put someone's life at risk," Som-kway said.

"My mother used some of these plants, but she

didn't say prayers over them. Why don't you just teach me each of the plants and their uses? Why don't we forget the chants?"

"There is knowledge for you to learn if you desire to learn it. There is a way to joy. I can pass on the ancient ways to you, but I must give you that marvelous bird's egg in its shell. If I give you just the egg, it will slip through your hands and will be useless to everyone."

I did not fully appreciate what Som-kway said to me that day, but as time went on, her words made more sense. I remembered that my mother certainly had her own rituals and songs. A hymn in church must not be so very different from a chant out in the woods. Could it be that each religion was its own kind of eggshell or container?

"Do you want to become a medicine woman?" I asked Sa-kat one day.

"Yes," she replied. "Don't you?"

"It's a lot of work," I said.

"You're lazy!"

How could I explain my feelings? I wanted to be a medicine woman, yet I felt I should not want it. Learning about plants was interesting, even though it was tedious at times. But at any moment I could leave the village to return to a completely different life.

"Pay attention!" Som-kway often scolded. I touched everything with shaking hands. I saw my mother's face everywhere. I lapsed into daydreams. I could not seem to hold my hands steady. I was always dropping things. Once I accidentally dropped one of Som-kway's largest and finest clay cooking pots, and it broke into five large pieces.

Was my family thinking about me as I was thinking

about them? I wondered. Had the Dutchman contacted them? Were they expecting me?

Som-kway showed me how to fashion new pots by molding the clay in holes in the ground and decorating them with impressions made from a cord-wrapped paddle. We wove baskets, too, from reeds in the lagoon.

Sa-kat and I worked side by side, making salves and pounding dried roots into powders. We brewed sassafras leaves and birch bark for healing drinks. Som-kway told us one day about a special salve for seeing in the dark. Such a plant, she said, was rare, and we would be very lucky if we were to find one in our lifetime.

Sa-kat and I did not find any of those plants, but sometimes Som-kway took us to a tiny promontory adjoining Two Island. There, fused into the gray boulders, were beautiful glistening rocks that were pink and white with flecks of shiny black. We chipped away small pieces of these magical rocks and put them into our pouches to give us luck and ward off evil spirits.

One day I nibbled on a mushroom among Som-kway's supplies. It was brown and small, like the other mushrooms, but it turned out to be poisonous. I felt a heaviness in my throat. Som-kway came a little nearer and leaned forward.

"Is this what you ate?" she asked.

I nodded.

She gave me a strong hot drink and a cup of salt water that made me vomit. She repeated the treatment many times over the next few days. I felt dizzy and tired, but within a week I was cured.

The poison mushroom seemed proof to me that my mother would not have approved of Som-kway's teaching. I wanted to convince myself of this, so that it would be easier for me to rejoin my own people.

"Why did you collect this kind of mushroom if it was so dangerous?" I asked her.

"There is a use for every type of plant," she answered. "Just because we can't eat a plant, that doesn't mean it isn't useful. We must learn to work with all that we have and not to exclude anything."

• • •

Another spring had passed. It had been about four months since I'd spoken to the Dutchman. Surely he had contacted Edward or Bridget or Faith.

But was Pieter Van Hook to be trusted? He could lead me to my brothers and sisters, or he could take me somewhere else. He could even sell me to another tribe! My snapping turtle looked at me anxiously in my dreams. I began to hope that the Dutchman would not return.

In summer the villagers were not expected to live by the natural routine and discipline we had in the winter. When the water grew warm enough for swimming, it was time for Sa-kat and me to join the children and dig for clams and paddle about in our dugout canoes.

The group of children was the same group of the year before. Now we were older, all eleven, twelve, or thirteen years old, and stronger and more independent than we'd been the previous summer.

We would paddle a few strokes, then skim at a fair speed over the rocky shallows of the lagoon. I loved my dugout canoe. I also loved to race over the clear, stony water and smell the fragrant pine trees. My hair, quite long now, was usually thick and stiff with salt water.

Sometimes the waves rose up and the trees filled with wind. We paddled to shore as fast as we could before the rains pelted down. The summer brought many thunderstorms. "It's the *pet-hak-hoo-way-ok,* huge birds with human heads, who flapped their wings," Som-kway taught me. "The young thunder beings fill the sky with the loudest thunder, the older thunder beings with deep, low rumbling." The thunder beings gave us rain.

I looked up into the sky in awe, hoping for a glimpse of these fearsome spirits. At the same time I prayed to God: *Bless the souls of my loved ones. Take me to my family.*

The boys liked to shoot birds with their bows and arrows. Once Tu-ma shot a cormorant just for sport. News of this conquest reached the elders of the village. Tu-ma and Chah-kol's mother, Kee-kee-cheem-wes, cooked the bird, and even though it had a sour taste and was not usually eaten, Tu-ma was forced to eat it. It would teach him a lesson about respecting animals and not wasting food, Kee-kee-cheem-wes said.

Clamming off a tiny island at the tip of the Place of Seashells, my friends and I found a child's skeleton buried deep among some rocks. Its moldy color suggested it had been there for years.

"Is it white or Indian?" I asked.

Chah-kol said the skeleton was an Indian boy's because of the stone amulet he wore around his neck. We carried the skeleton back to the elders of the village and had a ceremony for it at our people's graveyard.

I sang the Lenape ritual chants for the boy and only later realized I had forgotten to add my own Christian prayers.

The Place of Pigeons

CHAH-KOL POINTED TO A HUMPED GREEN island that was far away.

"That's the Place of Pigeons, where there's an abandoned village," he said.

The island was given its name because enormous flocks of pigeons were said to stay on it in the spring and fall. None of the children my age had dared paddle so far out.

"Let's go!" someone said.

All the boys and a few of the girls jumped into their canoes. I wanted to go with Sa-kat in her canoe but found she had already left with someone else. Why hadn't she waited for me? I paddled out with Tu-ma. I sat in the front of the canoe and Tu-ma took the rear. It was hard work.

We passed by a number of small islands, some that had two or three trees on them and others that were only gray boulders and rocks.

At last the length of the island appeared ahead of us, wide and green, with a small sandy beach and many massive gray boulders. We beached the canoe and ambled along the rocks to the other side of the island. The group was swimming and sunning themselves. Some had packed corn bread and water.

Chah-kol cheerfully offered me some corn bread. The other children danced and splashed in the water. After a while I realized Sa-kat was not with our group. I asked Chah-kol where she was.

"She and Kee-tak are exploring the abandoned wigwams in the woods," he said. I wondered why he suddenly seemed so knowing and so smug.

I pushed my way through the thick brush. The woods had reclaimed the old village; only a few huts were left standing. I poked my head into one, then another.

Suddenly I was aware of Sa-kat and Kee-tak at the other side of an entranceway, watching me. They sat together with their arms around one another.

In shock, I stood there, not knowing what to do.

"Mee-pahk!" Sa-kat called out. She looked startled.

I turned and ran back through the woods, stumbling and scratching myself against briars, until I reached the beach.

"You look as though you've seen a witch," Tu-ma said.

In silence I joined the others on the rocks. The day passed slowly. After a while Sa-kat and Kee-tak returned from the woods. I felt full of melancholy and brooding, as if she had in some way betrayed me.

On the journey back to Place of Stringing Beads island, paddling with Tu-ma, I thought of the way the Lenape liked to touch each other. They slept close together at times, leaning and pressing, or groping for each other in the dark.

That would be one good reason for returning to my family.

My own family had not acted in this way. Or had they? I had forgotten aspects of life with my old family. Perhaps I had wanted to forget. Suddenly the world seemed to me a very different place from the one I had first imagined. Had I been tricked or deceived over the years?

Surely my mother had known about the mysteries of life. She'd given birth so many times: I'd had six brothers and five sisters, but there were others who had died. At sixteen Annie had been considered a bit young to be a bride; perhaps my parents would have preferred that she wait until she was eighteen. But the Lenape . . . some of them were only thirteen when they wed!

Once at home, I got out of my wet clothes and dried myself. The sweet odors of *sa-pan* and corn bread wafted across the clearing. As I was wolfing down some of the bread, I saw Sa-kat approaching between the trees.

"Mee-pahk, you are angry with me."

I did not answer her directly. "Since when are you spending time with Kee-tak?"

She didn't reply.

"Do you like him?" I asked.

"Yes," she said.

"Why?"

"I just do," she answered. Her eyes were dark and beautifully shaped; now they seemed to glow. After a long pause, she continued. "Mee-pahk, soon you and I will begin our fertile cycles. Then we will marry."

Beneath my damp hair my scalp tingled. Cold air seemed to brush against the back of my legs.

"Are you going to marry Kee-tak?"

"I don't know."

"I don't want you to."

"We will always be sisters," Sa-kat said.

I sighed and tried to give Sa-kat a smile.

That night I found that my lower arms were so sore from paddling that I could not untie a bundle or pick up anything. I couldn't even help to gather firewood. Sa-kat said her arms ached, too, but she carried on with her work, more cheerfully than usual.

"Come here," Som-kway said to me. She had me lie down on the floor of the long house, then leaned and pressed on me. I felt the palms of her good, strong hands. She moved her hands on the tenderest parts of my arms, and I screamed out. Heat seemed to pour out of my arms and back. I felt a little better, but the pain was still so great, I couldn't sleep much that night.

The next day Som-kway stretched out my aching muscles again and I felt much better. She gave me a special hot broth. When we were alone in the long house, I asked her, "Why is it that Lenape girls marry so much younger than the English girls?"

"Do they?" she said. "I didn't know that."

"The English girls are usually eighteen years or older," I said.

"So you think it odd that the Lenape girls marry when they're thirteen or fourteen winters old?"

"Yes," I said. "I think it's wrong."

"Why is it wrong?" she asked.

I couldn't answer.

"*Ha!* I think you are troubled because you are only a winter or two away from marriage."

That was exactly what frightened me. I had lived

with the Lenape for nearly two years. I had always sup-posed I would be back with my own family long before now.

"You and Sa-kat are growing up," Som-kway said proudly.

"When I reach my fertile period, are you going to force me to marry?" I asked.

"No one will force you. It will be your decision."

Som-kway's words relieved me a little, but in the following days many worries clouded my mind. Sa-kat, in addition to having thick, beautiful hair, was now developing breasts. Much to my disappointment—and also a little to my relief—my chest remained completely flat. Sa-kat was so good-natured that she did not see my envy.

"You're wearing a lot of jewelry," I observed. Suk-ee-loon-gawn and some of the other women had given Sa-kat gifts. Everyone knew, without saying, that my friend was approaching maturity. She now wore several shell necklaces, a pendant, rings, and bangles, and her long hair was fastened behind her ears with a beaded cord. I thought she was becoming aware of her beauty, but she was not arrogant.

"Here," she said. She took off several of her bangles and necklaces. I covered my flat chest with the neck-laces and felt even more ashamed of my jealousy.

Everyone in our group was changing. Tu-ma wore a mark on his forehead, symbolizing our own clan, the Turtle people. The boys now carried full-sized bows. In the fall it would be time for them to go off by them-selves to receive their visions, as all Lenape men did.

Would I escape before it was time for me to marry a Lenape boy?

One day, when I was gathering raspberries in bark buckets with Sa-kat, she suddenly called out, "It happened! It happened!"

She told me her fertile period had started, and I was even more jealous of her.

When we returned to the village, Som-kway and Suk-ee-loon-gawn took her down to the beach and dunked her in the water a few times. They gathered moss for her to tie between her legs to absorb the blood. The berries she had picked were thrown away in the woods for the birds to eat, while mine were taken into the long house.

Sa-kat went to stay in the women's hut for a week because of the belief that the *ma-nu-too-wuk* hovered over menstruating women. I visited her there every day.

"Does it hurt?"

"No," she said.

"When my sisters had their monthly cycle, they'd never go off to a separate house like this," I said.

"Why not?" she asked.

"They just didn't. No one thought there were evil spirits hanging about."

Despite what I said about the evil spirits, Sa-kat ate the corn bread I'd given her with a sharpened wooden stick, as she had been instructed to do. She feared that otherwise the evil spirits would contaminate the food.

"What's happening back at the village? I'm bored here," Sa-kat said after she had been in the women's hut for about three days.

"Not a thing," I said. "Som-kway cured a few toothaches. The boys brought back some ducks from their hunt."

Conversation was awkward. "I wish I was having my monthly cycle too," I finally said.

"Nothing much happens," she said, her full lips in a pout. But I didn't believe her. When Sa-kat returned to the village, she was more confident and even more radiantly beautiful. She was flushed and elated, as if with a secret understanding.

After that, I began checking myself for blood. Nothing. I would not yet have to worry about marriage.

Pieter Van Hook

THE DAYS OF LATE SUMMER CONTINUED AS usual, and the hot sun soon ripened the corn. Harvest time had arrived once more. The men began to build the threshing houses. Two years had passed since I had first come to the Lenape, and it had been about eight months since I'd seen Pieter Van Hook. Soon I would be twelve years old. With every day that passed I grew a little closer to the possibility that I would have to stay and marry into the tribe.

Then one cold fall day a stranger in Lenape dress entered the palisades of our village. He had hairy skin, a dirty cloak, and narrow, unfocused eyes. Pieter Van Hook. At last!

The villagers greeted him.

Wam-pak greeted him. "You are without your people, the Wappingers," Wam-pak said.

"Sometimes I travel alone, sometimes with others," the Dutchman said. "It is easier that I go alone when I go to New Amsterdam."

He no longer had his head shaved in the style of the Lenape; now his hair grew in thin tufts. He was older than I had remembered. Forty-five? Fifty? He had the same crazed, angry expression. I did not like him. Had he come to rescue me, or had he come for another reason?

Pieter Van Hook carried white men's fishhooks and knives. He traded goods with Wam-pak and the elders. At first the Dutchman pretended not to notice me.

Would he ask me to leave the village with him? *Oh, Lord in heaven, I have gotten myself into a terrible situation,* I thought. *Mother, what would you have me do?*

If I decided not to go with the Dutchman, would I ever find a way back to my family?

The best thing to do was to wait, I decided. I would find a way to talk to him.

That evening Wam-pak gave Pieter Van Hook shelter in one of our huts. But Wam-pak was not fooled by the Dutchman. Late at night, when Sa-kat and I were supposed to be sleeping, we overheard Wam-pak talking to Som-kway outside our long house. "He says he is a friend of the Wappingers. He fought with them, but now he travels alone."

"The man is not to be trusted. I see that he has too much white above the pupils of his eyes," Som-kway said.

"He says he wants to marry Mee-pahk and take her back with him to the Wappinger village. He offers twenty fishhooks for her, in addition to the goods he has already traded with us."

I gasped and looked at Sa-kat. She held my hand tightly.

"*Koo!* No, absolutely not!" Som-kway returned. "I would not have Mee-pahk go with this man. Even if he were to be trusted, Mee-pahk is still too young. Besides, she is your daughter, Wam-pak. You took her and you should be responsible for her. I want her near us."

I felt such relief. Did the Dutchman truly intend to marry me? He was so old and so ugly! If returning to my home meant marrying this man, I would never go with him. Was he trying to deceive me or Wam-pak?

The next morning I awoke with my teeth clenched. I lay on my sleeping platform, my eyes squeezed shut, unable to move.

Perhaps I could hide myself until Pieter Van Hook left the village.

Already that morning Som-kway, Suk-ee-loon-gawn, and Wam-pak had left the long house to talk to the elders.

I decided to pick mushrooms on the outskirts of Place of Stringing Beads village, not far from the pine grove. "I'll go with you," Sa-kat said. "But we'll need to bring Mee-kwun. I must watch him."

"No. I want to go alone."

My heart thumped as I ran, and I dropped the basket I was carrying. I would find it later. When I reached the pine groves, I realized I had made a mistake. I should have stayed in the village. I should have found Som-kway and Wam-pak and stayed with them.

I turned back. I was almost to the village when I saw him, coming through the trees. His face was painted. His soiled cloak dragged on the ground, and his head looked patchy. It was bald in some places and had long blondish brown hair in others.

The man walked slowly toward me. His clothes smelled moldy. The Lenape smelled of grease and smoke, but they did not wear damp or decaying skins or furs.

My body trembled.

What would he do to me? I had brought trouble on myself. Maybe others, too.

He rushed forward and I shrieked. He grabbed my arm.

"Let me go!" I screamed.

"Do you still want to be traded back to your family?"

"Have you contacted any of my brothers or sisters?"

"We will do that later. There are many problems at the fort just now. I told the officers of the matter, but they didn't listen. I couldn't find any messengers. The Dutch West India Company has told Governor Kieft that he will be replaced. We will have to wait."

"If I go with you, where will you take me?"

"To the fort, but first we must visit a few other Lenape villages where I have business."

I did not like the way he stared at me. Som-kway was right about his eyes; there was something sinister about them. Had he lied about the messengers? Perhaps he had never visited the fort in the first place.

"I have pretended to Wam-pak that I will marry you," he continued.

"Wam-pak will not allow it," I said.

"Then we must run away! Tonight, just after dark. Meet me where your villagers keep their canoes."

I bit my lower lip. What should I say?

"I'm staying here," I said firmly.

"Stupid girl! Meet me after sunset or you will die with the Indians. I'm going to set a ring of fire around the village tonight!"

"*Koo!*" I yelled, horrified.

I tried to run away, but he held me back. With one

147

arm he grabbed for something in the pouch he was carrying. He pointed a knife at my throat and said, "I thought you were like my own daughter. I realize now that you're like these savages. You've become one of them!"

The knife still at my throat, I lowered myself to a squatting position. I reached down and threw some sand into his eyes, then ran. He chased after me, but I knew the shortcuts between the trees. Shrieking, I raced back through the woods to the village. "Wam-pak!" I called. I glanced behind me to find that the man was gone.

I ran right into Suk-ee-loon-gawn, nearly knocking her over with her baby on her back.

We found Wam-pak repairing a fishnet at the lagoon with a few of the warriors. He gathered Mah-kwa, Som-kway, and other elders. I told them what Pieter Van Hook planned to do. The men organized search parties. The villagers spread out in groups to find him. I refused to leave Sa-kat's side for the rest of the day. I was so shaken, I needed to be held.

It was a cool late-summer afternoon. A breeze pushed pink and gray clouds across the sky. But on the mainland, black clouds rose up above the trees. The strong, bitter smell of charred trees filled the air.

Someone screamed. "The stranger has set fire to our cornfields!"

Som-kway turned pale. She looked old and full of sorrow. I could see that some terrible danger lay ahead. The whole sky turned scarlet. The water turned red in reflection. Darkness never came that night.

The women and girls had worked hard to plant the crops. It was the labor of two seasons.

The fire burned on the mainland for two days until a sudden rainstorm put it out. Parts of the hunting ground were now charred and desolate. Nearly half of the corn was gone. More land would need to be cleared to plant.

I crept away to hide. Would Pieter Van Hook have come back to the village without my encouragement? Hadn't I been responsible for Suk-ah-sun's death? Was I responsible for this new hardship? The villagers did not blame me, but I still felt guilty. I had hoped for a clean way to escape without harming them.

I thought about what Som-kway had meant by a divided heart.

The *Gamwing* Ceremony

"PEACE HAS BEEN DECLARED!" WAM-PAK announced a few weeks later.

Wappinger and Wiechquaeskeck emissaries delivered the news. Everyone in the village feasted, drummed, and paraded. I learned that Governor Kieft had traveled from Manhattan to Fort Orange on the North River to sign a treaty with all the Lenape Indians in New Netherland. Included in the peace treaty were representatives of the Wappingers, Wiechquaeskeck, Hackensack, Tappan, and Canarsee, as well as our own people, the Siwanoy, and other Lenape bands on either side of the river.

The peace had come just in time, because it meant that boys in my group would not be going to war.

That fall Chah-kol and Tu-ma left for their vision quests together. The elders had decided that the boys were so much alike that the *ma-nu-too-wuk* wished them to remain companions in all stages of life. Perhaps in the spirit world their souls had once been separated and missed each other; now, on earth, they grew like two trees together.

As other fathers did that fall, Mah-kwa took his sons

into the thick woods off our island. He left them in two separate places, without any food to eat, but checked on them daily. Tu-ma returned the third morning, proud and smiling. Chah-kol returned that evening. The boys were then allowed to go off on a hunting trip by themselves up the river in the canoe they had made. During the trip, the boys entered into the glowing light of a rainbow, which Som-kway said was a blessed sign.

I marveled at the way the villagers could accept their difficult lives. We harvested the remaining corn that had not been destroyed in the fire with little complaint about the damage. We gathered more fish than usual to compensate for the loss of corn, beans, and squash.

I decided it was time to push away the hope of returning to my family. Why, after two years had gone by, should I keep hoping? I would try to be happy. When I missed my family, I would try to bury my feelings.

In preparation for the *gamwing*, the men added new bark to the roof of the ceremonial lodge at Mishow Rock. The elders gave Tu-ma, now a skilled artist, the honor of carving two new posts bearing the face of Mu-sing. Tu-ma carved the masks on the living trees so that the masks, too, would have life. Som-kway appointed Sa-kat and me as ceremonial attendants and we strewed the floor of the Big House with new cattail mats we had woven over the summer.

Back at the village we pounded cornmeal; then we baked bread, wrapped in cornhusks and placed deep inside the fire's ashes. A few days before the festival the men and boys went off hunting. What a feast we would have!

On the morning of the ceremony Sa-kat and I bathed in a cold spring. Som-kway had the hot rocks for the sweat lodge ready for us when we returned. All of us prepared and purified our bodies before we covered ourselves with bear grease to ward off mosquitoes and to make our skin shiny. I remembered how once I had thought Indians were dirty and never cleaned themselves. Now I knew otherwise.

Lovely Sa-kat! She now had very long, even fuller hair. When she laughed, she had a beautiful, open smile. I was proud that she was my sister. For the festival we would wear our best wraparound skirts decorated with quills and beadwork and drape iridescent turkey-feather robes about our shoulders. In my new clothes I felt less scrawny, even pretty.

Suk-ee-loon-gawn kept coming up with things for me to do. "You! Find my pendant!" she would say, or "Repair my moccasins!" I no longer found her sharpness so threatening. It was just part of who she was.

Finally the evening of the *gamwing* ceremony arrived. I walked with Sa-kat and some of the younger children to the ceremonial lodge at Mishow Rock.

The night was dark and full of stars. The drumming had already begun, and the orange fires and torches burned. We entered a sacred space that loomed out of the night, mysterious and glowing. I followed Sa-kat around to the far corner of the large, square room. The drummers congregated near the center post. My eyes stung a little as I breathed in the dry, pungent smoke. Shadows danced on the walls, and the carved faces on the posts seemed to sway and move as if they were alive.

I looked for Chah-kol and Tu-ma as a group of boys entered. Tu-ma opened the skin door very carefully and blushed a little. Tu-ma, Chah-kol, and Kee-tak had had all the hair plucked from their heads, except for a spiky crest at the top, which was greased and tied with a turkey feather. They seemed different—it wasn't just the hair—and I couldn't help staring at them.

Mah-kwa, wearing bear fur and the fearsome black-and-red Mu-sing mask, danced and shook his rattle. I was not afraid of the mask now.

Som-kway led the ceremonies, assisted by Mah-kwa. She made the opening remarks. "We are assembled here in the Big House ready for our time of worship. The Big House has been made clean for Kee-shay-lu-moo-kawng, who is with us now. We thank him for all the things on this earth that we enjoy, for he made them all."

Som-kway gazed at the onlookers with a wide, transfixed grin. Her eyes seemed oddly large and radiant.

She threw some tobacco on the fire and chanted in a subdued voice as she gave thanks for all the animals we hunted and also the many plants we ate or used to cure illnesses. As Som-kway chanted she waved her fan of eagle feathers over the fire. I watched with awe as a column of pungent smoke rose up through the hole at the center of the Big House roof; it was being carried directly to the heavens.

We drank a bitter drink made from dried berries, passing a cup from one to another; then the vision dances followed. I sat on the floor cross-legged, my fringed skirt over my knees, while the men danced and sang. I felt dreamy and dazed with the warmth all around me. Children nestled at my feet. A few old people in the corner were like shrunken corpses, with wrinkled faces pinched, their eyes half open.

Each man feverishly shook the turtle-shell rattle as he chanted. Mah-kwa sang his bearlike song; then Wam-pak told the story of a great white chestnut tree with wide, spreading branches. Under this tree he had seen a snake.

Kee-tak, with his deep booming voice, mimicked a wolf howling to the full moon. Sa-kat eyed him with complete adoration.

Finally it was time to hear Chah-kol and Tu-ma. Happiness and excitement flushed over Tu-ma's small face as he entered into his story.

> "High in the air
> Soaring, gliding
> Circling around and around
> Shrewd, deliberate
> Sharp little eyes
> Spot the tiny mouse
> Swooping down, down
> Long, curved talons
> Grab that mouse
> Tasty, juicy
> Bones and fur
> Eat him up!
> Eat him up!"

Tu-ma spread out his arms like a hawk; he suddenly jumped up, then crouched down on the ground to enact the kill. It took me by surprise, so I giggled and pinched Sa-kat.

Chah-kol cleared his throat. Then he began to shake the turtle rattle and tell his vision in a singsong way.

His voice was both gentle and loud. I watched him force his shoulders back a few times as he sang.

> "Small and brown
> He flits about on rounded wings
> I catch a glimpse of his large,
>   white tail patches
> He winters far away
> His is the voice in the night woods
> The voice in the night woods
> His voice rolling
> Tirelessly repeating
> Whip-poor-will! Whip-poor-will!"

Chah-kol cleverly trilled the whippoorwill's call; he had a talent for birdcalls. The crowd clapped, stomped their feet, and shook their rattles. Kee-kee-cheem-wes beamed with pride.

Next all the men danced, and Chah-kol joined in shyly, bounding along. I knew he felt relieved that his vision telling was over. Then all of us chanted the prayer call twelve times, *"Hoo-oooooooo!"*, letting our voices extend and harmonize. It surprised me how deep and resonant my voice could be when I chanted, as I had never been one to carry a tune when I had lived with my birth family.

At midnight we feasted; I filled my stomach with striped bass, beaver tail, and sweet deer meat cooked with chestnuts.

The *gamwing* ceremony lasted twelve nights. Every sunset I renewed my excitement for the night's festivities.

On the twelfth and final night it was time for the

women and girls to dance. I looked over my shoulder and copied Sa-kat. Som-kway recited a vision she'd had and encouraged me to share one of my visions as well. I was proud to be the only girl asked to recite a vision.

This time I decided I would sing. I was to be a medicine woman. I wanted everyone in the village to know of my talents.

When my turn came, I climbed over the rows of knees to go to the center of the room. I clutched the turtle rattle in my hand and planted my feet firmly on the ground, as Som-kway had taught me. I sang under my breath in short, nervous pants.

"I am old
I have undergone hardships
Grooves on my back
Round back
Small red eyes
Mud, the winter
Down under
Very still
Very still
Lie in wait
Fish swim by
Snap! Snap!
Can you guess who I am?"

After my song I looked about me. My heart beat rapidly. My knees felt weak. I thought of Mother, the fear and the anger she stirred in people. For one terrible moment I wished I had not gotten up in front of the crowd.

My gaze moved from one person to another: to Wam-pak, Sa-kat, Suk-ee-loon-gawn, Som-kway, Chah-kol, Tu-ma. They all looked proud and happy. Then everyone in the Big House congratulated me. More than ever, I felt a part of my Lenape family.

Falling in Love

GENERALLY THE BOYS DIDN'T TALK VERY much to the girls. Chah-kol was the exception. He would talk at length, and with anyone; I loved his stories.

Ever since he had given me my canoe, we had been friends. But shortly after the *gamwing* ceremony, my feelings changed. I was putting dried foods into a storage pit when he came over to chat with me. Chah-kol had grown into a new form and was more of a man now, I thought, though his walk was still bobbing and boyish.

Chah-kol aspired to be a great deer hunter. Mahkwa and the chief hunters of the tribe were initiating him into their secrets. They had given Chah-kol his own designated hunting ground.

"Great hunters must have patience," he told me. "Once I waited in the same place for a whole day, hardly moving, until a big buck came right up to me. The heavier the cover, the closer the deer get to you. The buck was as close to me as I am to you right here. I drew my bow back and aimed right for his chest! I nearly got him!"

He squinched his nose up a bit and enlarged his nostrils. This expression made me laugh.

On this day and many other days Chah-kol boasted of his new knowledge. It was all talk. After hunting with the men for a year, he had not yet killed a deer.

Gradually I realized a startling fact: Chah-kol's hunting territory was the place where my family had lived. The sun-warmed fields and the gentle rising ground, where Chah-kol said the deer fanned out to graze, must be the very spot where our house had stood. The nearby swamps and dense brush where the deer bedded were where I used to gather water with my sisters. But I did not begrudge Chah-kol this land. If any of the villagers was to have it, I wanted it to be him.

I watched the lines form at the corners of Chah-kol's mouth when he talked. His cheeks flushed. I was oddly quiet; all I wanted to do was listen to him. "The hunter knows the warm spots in the forest that are teeming with life and the cold spots in the forest where the snow is last to melt, where the deer do not go. . . . All the elders say that the greatest moments a hunter ever experiences are the times he spends alone."

I held Chah-kol's bow once when he wasn't looking. It was much heavier than it appeared. His long, slim fingers were callused from the string of this giant bow. What did Chah-kol think of me? There were many things I longed to say. I worked up the courage to tell him about a dream. "I saw a frog just about to leap, and I think it means you will do great things in your life." He smiled bashfully and said that his real name, given by Som-kway, meant One Who Walks in the Lead.

I realized I was falling in love and held the secret close to me for a few weeks. Chah-kol was of the Turtle clan, and he could only marry a girl who was a Wolf or a Turkey. But I didn't care. I couldn't wait until night-fall to be alone and free to stare up at the ceiling of the long house and think about him.

All day I felt lifted up and joyful. The colors of the sky seemed more intense. I listened to the wind rise up suddenly and rustle the brilliant flame leaves. I watched the water moving restlessly, sometimes slate blue, gray, or deep blue, depending on the sky above. I noticed the crisscrossing of deer tracks in the mud and thought of Chah-kol. I was happy to go about my chores and even added to them. I made some new pottery jars for Som-kway and Suk-ee-loon-gawn. I even fashioned some tiny faces in the designs here and there. When Chah-kol left for a few days on a hunting trip, I made him a rabbit-fur jacket to keep myself from missing him too much.

One day I was gathering chestnuts with Sa-kat and chanced upon Chah-kol in his hunting outfit: leggings, belt, a fur cloak wrapped over one shoulder to leave his right arm free, his bird-skin pouch hanging from his neck. He moved among the trees not far from our vil-lage, shooting at targets with Tu-ma.

As we drew closer, I could see that the brothers had fashioned their own full-sized buck out of grasses and sticks. Its realistic round chestnut eyes and twiggy ant-lers impressed me. It was like them to create something so witty.

Chah-kol balanced his limbs to get the right pull but shot too fast. His arrow wobbled in the air and fell a few feet from the made-up deer. Then the boys noticed Sa-kat and me.

"Go away! We are doing important work here!" Tu-ma said.

"No girls allowed!" Chah-kol joined in.

Sa-kat smiled when she saw the shape of the target. We all knew how important it was to Chah-kol that he bring in a deer.

Leaning against an oak tree, I continued to gaze at Chah-kol. I had developed a nervous giggling habit that I hated. Chah-kol looked at us for a moment but then fastened his eyes on the target again. His losses did not dampen his enthusiasm. That was one thing I liked about him.

But soon after, I began to notice that Chah-kol rarely listened to me, not the way I did to him. I wasn't quite so sympathetic about his yearning to succeed as a hunter.

Then as fall turned into winter and the last of the leaves fell to the ground, the feel of the air took me back to the time when I had first mourned my mother, brothers, and sisters. I suddenly recalled details about them. Kate's face flashed before me. I talked to her in English, as if she could hear me.

I cried sometimes without knowing why, and I did not want to spend time with Som-kway. Worse, I pushed Sa-kat away.

About this time I discovered some solace in going to the northwestern beach of the island and climbing up on that big boulder, the Gray Mare. I'd disliked that side of the island ever since the incident when the children had made fun of me. But now I had grown to appreciate that the shoreline was so muddy that hardly anyone ever went there, especially not in winter.

On the rock one afternoon, bundled in furs, I lay for hours thinking of Chah-kol, trying to sort out my feelings. The wind drove the surf violently, making it pound and break. I stayed on the rock almost until the tide had changed from high to low. I absorbed the wet, salty air. I liked the view from this place: two dark, thin rocky reefs ahead of me and two larger islands.

I put my face up toward the sun and felt its warmth, turning away from the wind. I felt a little better, and I climbed back down the rock and occupied myself for a few minutes pressing the toe of my moccasin into the mud wherever I saw bubbles appear. In this area there were a lot of clams that shot a small jet of water at you when you stepped on them. By the time I returned to the village it was nearly sunset.

"Where have you been?" Sa-kat asked. She had already prepared the fires, although it had been my turn to sweep out the ashes and collect new firewood.

I shrugged.

"I'd like to know what's the matter with you!" Sa-kat went on. "Som-kway would like to know, too. I think she's out right now finding herbs to make a potion for you."

A few months had gone by since the *gamwing* ceremony, and I was now ready to open a part of my heart to her.

"It's Chah-kol!" I said. "All he does is talk about himself, but if I have something to say, he doesn't listen."

"So? He's always like that."

"He says I'm quiet," I went on. "He doesn't know me."

"*You,* quiet? *Ha!*" Sa-kat said, and laughed. "You're right. He doesn't know you."

Even I had to laugh at that.

"I don't like Chah-kol anymore. He's only interested in himself!"

"*Ha!* Chah-kol is a boy. What do you expect?" Sa-kat said good-naturedly.

"I dislike all boys and men," I lied. "I'm in no hurry for Som-kway to marry me off. There isn't a single Wolf or Turkey boy who interests me. What about you? Do you still have feelings for Kee-tak?"

"I don't know," Sa-kat answered, a bit mischievously.

"Are you spending time with him?"

"No, not much. I have some other suitors."

"Who?" I demanded.

Sa-kat mentioned the names of two of Wam-pak's braves, grown men, hunters and warriors. I was surprised, though perhaps I should not have been.

She wouldn't tell me any more.

It was good to talk to Sa-kat again, but I sensed she would only gradually let me back into her life, since I had shut her out of mine for so long.

"Why do you complain so much? What more do you want than you have already?" Sa-kat said, a bit angry now. "I listen to you. I listen to every word you say, don't I? Som-kway listens to you. Everyone in the village pays attention to you. You're the only girl who has visions, and somehow you think that because of this, you don't have to work as hard as the rest of us!"

I hadn't realized Sa-kat was jealous for never having had a vision. *Isn't it strange,* I thought, *for Sa-kat to wish she could be more like me, when I wish I could be more like her?*

"I'm sorry I haven't been a better friend to you lately," I said.

Som-kway entered the long house with some roots and twigs. That night she boiled the plants down into a greenish brown medicine, which she made me swallow the next morning. The medicine must have worked, because in the following weeks I thought about Chah-kol much less, was happier, and felt more a part of the village again.

Chah-kol and the other young men and boys left on a long hunting trip soon after the first snowfall. My heart sank. As the weeks went by, I stopped expecting him. My lovesickness drained away from me. I devoted myself to collecting firewood because I knew our village would soon have a great need for it. The snow fell, white and heavy against the dark trees, leaving huge drifts. It snowed and snowed. Sa-kat and I organized the children of the village to dig out paths between the wigwams.

A few times I ventured out on my snowshoes to walk in the bright, glistening woods. Some bitterly cold days followed, and we all crouched near the two fires inside the long house. We had begun to draw supplies from our inside storage pits now, cornmeal to blend into *sa-pan,* and dried fish and meat. Som-kway was often tired, and she developed a bad cough. I feared for her. I also began to fear that something must have happened to our men and boys. Had the Dutch killed them?

I tried to be patient.

Then one day the boys and men returned, loudly

whooping and calling, and laden down with bloody game, which they dragged over the snow on wooden frames. I ran toward them on my snowshoes. There were more dead animals than I had ever seen. The men had even hunted down an enormous brown bear! And when I looked at Chah-kol's proud face, I knew that he had killed his first deer.

Tricks and Wood Dwarves

I WAS SO INTENT ON BUTCHERING THE GAME that I did not notice Wam-pak beside me.

"*Nee-chan,*" he said, addressing me as his daughter.

"*He,*" I greeted him in return, not looking at him. I began to cut the meat into strips for smoking.

"You have grown into a young woman. I hardly recognize you!" he exclaimed.

Old feelings returned. I couldn't look at him easily.

"There is meat to fill our stomachs. There is fur to keep us warm," Wam-pak said.

"Yes," I replied flatly. "I will sew a new coat for Mee-kwun with this fur. The antlers will be useful for new tools for spring planting."

"Som-kway says you are becoming a good helper to her. You have become one of us. I hope you are content."

We looked at each other. Then I dropped my eyes. "Sometimes I am," I said slowly, "but because of you I don't know if I will ever find contentment."

"You will forget the past."

"I will never forget what you did to my family," I

said. I avoided his stare, yet I felt his presence strongly. I often felt Wam-pak's presence even when he traveled to distant hunting grounds.

Standing in Wam-pak's shadow, I wiped the blood from my hands with snow. I would always associate blood and death with him.

I looked up at last to find he'd gone.

• • •

The villagers slept soundly after the evening feast. Snow fell, a soft, tracking snow. Chah-kol and a few other young men went off to hunt again while the snow was still coming down. Now I saw him for what he was: an eager young hunter, my friend and my cousin.

Late winter was the time for the women to make maple syrup. We boiled the sap over a fire. Then we mixed it with bear fat to make a thick, sweet paste for our meat.

While I was stirring a pot of this sweet grease, I decided to confide in Som-kway. "I wanted Chah-kol to like me," I told her. "I thought about him all day long. Then when he finally came back from the hunt, it didn't matter to me anymore."

"It was fire," she said. "We are meant to have fire in us. It fuels us. We are not meant to stay in fire, however. After a while it turns and becomes something else."

"I suppose so," I said, trying to follow her. I thought that what she meant was that feelings, after a while, run their course.

"Think of the wave on the beach," Som-kway went on. "At first, in the sea, it is but a ripple. It gathers force. Then there is passion. There is no turning back! But then the wave breaks. It turns under. The passion is transformed. It goes back to sea and joins with the other waves."

"My mother had a lot of fire in her. Even my father used to say so," I said.

"From what you say, that seems right," Som-kway answered.

"Mother liked to argue. She made people angry and became well known as a troublemaker. That's why we moved all the time."

"It is good to have some fire in us. It is what shapes our lives and gives us purpose. At the same time, we must sometimes be careful to temper ourselves."

"Mother could have controlled her anger better. But she was a good person. She was strong. The ministers in our town frightened people with their tales of doom and punishment, and Mother wanted these people to think of God in a different way. I never told Mother I appreciated her. I wish I could now."

"I believe it would make your mother proud if you followed your own fires of the heart, without being overwhelmed or defeated by them."

"How is it that some people seem to stay in love with each other for a very long time, even for most of their lives? My parents were this way."

"I don't think it's possible for anyone to stay in love, not constantly. I think what happens is that we fall in and out of love and go in circles like spiraling waves of the sea. It is the going back and forth that solidifies us," Som-kway answered.

• • •

Spring was slow to come. For weeks there were howling, bitter winds that tore branches off the trees and formed high seas that crashed against the shore.

"Our Grandmother Where It Is Warm is arguing with Our Grandfather Where It Is Winter," Som-kway told me. "The *ma-nu-too-wuk* who guard the four quadrants of the earth roll stones in the sky and gamble with each other. This is what is happening when the seasons change."

I pictured Som-kway and her brother, Mah-kwa, two old ones teasing each other and rolling pebbles out of a bag on a winter's night.

At last the meadows of Laap-ha-wach-king bloomed with grasses and flowers, and the songs of birds increased. We planted the corn hills and helped the men with their fishing. Then Sa-kat and I accompanied Som-kway to find healing plants. We smeared grease on our bodies to keep away the mosquitoes as we gathered plants in the swamps.

Som-kway would not let me forget that all things— every plant, animal, and stone—had its own spirit, or *ma-nu-too*. For our medicines to be truly effective, she cautioned, the plants must be taken with their proper regard.

It was near a tall ironweed plant that I forgot the chant halfway through. "Go ahead, Mee-pahk. *A-lup-see!*" she said. "Hurry. It is waiting for its tobacco."

I did not care if I kept the plant waiting or not. "I can't remember things as you do," I said to Som-kway.

"You are lazy—and worse, you are not mindful! I excuse you as much as I can because you are young, but a Lenape person must not act so selfishly," she said. With that Som-kway chanted in her low voice, moaning between her teeth, to finish the song to the ironweed plant. She dug a little hole for it and reverently offered it a little tobacco from her bird-skin bag.

The next day two pimples appeared on my chin and another near my nose.

"See," Sa-kat said, "the ironweed plant was angry with you."

Soon after that I injured the middle finger on my right hand when I tripped and fell over a stone on one of the pathways near our village. I angrily kicked the stone into the woods. Immediately the end of my finger swelled up and turned purple. It was so sore that I could hardly do anything for about a week.

"The stone was angry at you for walking so arrogantly on its path," Som-kway said.

"Either that or you have offended the *wem-ah-tay-ku-hees-uk,* the wood dwarves," Sa-kat suggested.

Though I didn't quite believe in the wood dwarves, I looked about suspiciously whenever I walked in the woods. Once I thought I saw a little man dressed all in hides. Before I could take a good look at him, he hopped behind a tree.

Was I cursed with bad luck? I got lost in the woods. Then later, on my way home from gathering clams in my canoe, I moved through a place where the currents were strong and lost control of the boat. I spun around for several minutes before I could get my bearings. The canoe tipped and I fell into the cold water. It was after dark when I returned to the long house, soaked all the way through.

Suk-ee-loon-gawn wrapped me in my bearskin covering; she seemed surprisingly tender. Sa-kat coaxed me to swallow a drink she had made from elm bark strips.

I was in a miserable mood that night. I missed Mother and Kate and Annie. "I hate it here!" I said in my own language, which I now used only when I was so angry at my Lenape family that I wanted to shut them out.

"Kee-shay-lu-mee-eng, take pity on her," Som-kway said, offering a prayer to the Creator.

"Little Mee-pahk," she said, putting her arm around me, "you are out of balance, and everything is going wrong for you. I wish I could make you understand about our disciplines and rituals. It is our way. We learn the chants, we pay attention, we walk mindfully on the earth so we do not disturb the beings around us. Little by little our daily practices strengthen us. They become like good moccasins. We wear them and we can get through anything!"

Just then I heard an uneven whistling outside the long house. Someone was playing a flute. Then another flute began to play.

Sa-kat giggled and her cheeks flushed.

A voice called out, "Pretty Sa-kat! Come join us outside!" I recognized the deep voice as Kee-tak's.

Sa-kat gathered a fur cloak around her shoulders and slipped outside.

Suk-ee-loon-gawn beamed triumphantly. "I knew that my daughter would have many suitors. I hear not one flute but two flutes. . . . No, now I think I hear three flutes!"

Mee-kwun ran to go outside, but Suk-ee-loon-gawn stopped him. "Stay here. Don't bother them. Play with Mee-mun-dut," she said. She poured a sack of smooth stones onto the rushes of the floor to amuse him.

After a while Wam-pak came back from talking with

the men and entered our long house. He joined his wife in her merriment. Suk-ee-loon-gawn, Som-kway, and Wam-pak all drank hot sassafras water and chatted with each other as we listened to the flute music outside. I drank my own bowlful in silence.

"Three playing and not one of them can hold a tune!" Wam-pak said.

"Ha! You're right!" Suk-ee-loon-gawn answered. "You could play a better tune than that when you approached me with a love song, Wam-pak!"

"Not much better!" Wam-pak returned.

"Your flute playing was better than the first meals I made for you," Suk-ee-loon-gawn said in a rare moment of poking fun at herself. As everyone knew, Suk-ee-loon-gawn was too lazy to be much of a cook, though few women of the village could sew or stitch designs the way she could.

After a while I could only hear one flute. Sa-kat had evidently made her choice.

When I couldn't stand waiting any longer, I stood up, brushed the hide of the doorway aside, and stepped into the chill of the night. The flute playing had stopped. In the moonlight, right near a wigwam, I saw two figures sitting on the ground. They whispered and giggled. Perhaps they were kissing.

When I returned to the long house, the family had gone to sleep, except Wam-pak and Suk-ee-loon-gawn; they gazed at each other lovingly.

I lay down and thought about my flat chest, my pimples, my lank red hair, the sore on my finger, and the new poison ivy on my toes and knees. Sa-kat did not come inside for another hour.

The Pox

THE FALL I TURNED THIRTEEN, DISASTER came to our village, though the harvest season began like any other. Sa-kat and I and my little shadow, a younger girl called Aleech-kway, shared a threshing tent. I sat between them happily beating the corn with my bone awl until my arms were sore. The kernels separated from the cobs and fell to the bottom of the pile. Sometimes the kernels flew up in my face.

At the end of the day we went through the cobs to pick off any remaining kernels. The empty cobs were burned in bonfires.

Suk-ee-loon-gawn liked us to keep the ashes of the corncob fire pure of other debris. If the fire remained clean, the next day she would remove the crust, roll it into little grease balls, and use it to season the *sa-pan* and beans. Then Suk-ee-loon-gawn would have her fill of the smoke-flavored food she liked best.

It was almost impossible to keep our fires clean, however, because some of the boys had developed a game of throwing flaming mud balls. They would hold a mud ball on the end of a stick, which they dipped in our fire to ignite.

As dusk came and our work was finished, we made several big fires because there was no wind. Chah-kol and Tu-ma, young men now but still very boyish, held their mud balls high over their heads as they raced toward us.

"Don't go near the fire!" I warned.

"Pa-lee-ah!" Sa-kat screamed. "Get away!"

It was already too late. The boys swished past us, making loud whooping sounds like war cries. *"Ha! Ha! Ans-ha!* Dip it up!" With that, they stuck their mud balls into the fire and pulled out flaming torches. When the boys had run some distance from us, Chah-kol called out, "Watch out!" He hurled a ball in my direction. Other boys from the village joined in. Soon mud balls arched through the sky like shooting stars. Even little Mee-kwun took a mud ball and lit it. I snatched it away from him. He cried.

"Ku-la-mah-pee!" I said, telling him to behave.

"He is wild," Sa-kat said.

I looked around for Suk-ee-loon-gawn or Som-kway. Running, I pushed my way into our long house. Mah-kwa, Suk-ee-loon-gawn, Wam-pak, and several adults were talking.

Something told me that I should be quiet, but before I could stop myself, I blurted out, "Suk-ee-loon-gawn, your son is throwing flaming mud balls."

"Cheet-kwu-see! Won't this girl ever stop talking?" she snapped.

"We are having an important conversation here, Mee-pahk," Wam-pak said.

I tried to listen at the door as I was going out, but Som-kway and the others seemed determined not to talk until I was some distance away from them.

On the alert for flaming mud balls, I walked about the village. After some time I found Sa-kat, who was burning the last of the corncobs. "Mah-kwa and Som-kway are holding a meeting with the elders."

"What's happening?" Sa-kat asked, poking the fire with a stick. She looked anxious.

"I don't know," I said. "Your aunt told me to be quiet," I added.

Sa-kat sighed. "Try to get along with her."

"I've tried for years now! I give up," I said.

"Som-kway says that people who are bitter are people who have been terribly disappointed by others," Sa-kat said. "She said it's different for an adult like Suk-ee-loon-gawn to have an angry personality than for a child to have one. Children throw tantrums out of their ignorance. Older people are more entitled to their anger sometimes because they have lived many moons, seen many waves turn under."

"You're sounding like Som-kway," I said. "I wonder if we're going to war again."

"I hope not," Sa-kat answered.

What hit our village was an attack, but it wasn't war. A visitor from a tribe to the north brought the pox with him. It was the same disease that had claimed many members of the tribe several years before I had joined them. Soon a family on the opposite side of the village all became infected. Sa-kat and I mixed poultices of black-walnut bark, golden thread, and milkweed, but we were not allowed to accompany Som-kway on her visits. We gathered red cedar for her to burn. Tu-ma carved a new mask out of a living poplar tree for his father to use when healing. The boys forgot all about mud balls.

Red-and-black-faced Mu-sing visited the village in a bearskin with his turtle rattle. Though no one was much in the mood for the *gamwing* ceremony, Som-kway oversaw the twelve-day feasting. The only joyful thing that happened was that Suk-ee-loon-gawn's baby was now old enough to have his own name. We called him Es-pun, Raccoon.

"We have not upheld all the customs of the *gam-wing*," Som-kway said to Wam-pak one day. "When we had more participants, we performed the dances better. Years ago we had not one but many gatherings—Wolf, Turkey, and Turtle each with their own Big House. I fear we are a doomed people because we have offended the *ma-nu-too-wuk*."

"If we are a dying people, it is because of the white men," Wam-pak answered bitterly.

I sensed that he was right. Place of Stringing Beads village and probably other Lenape villages did not have populations large enough to sustain themselves when many people perished from war or disease.

By the time the first snow fell, more than twenty people in our village had died. We split up into groups of seven or eight for the winter, as Som-kway believed this would keep the disease from spreading. Wam-pak, Som-kway, and Mah-kwa stayed in the village to care for the sick. Most others moved from the village to return in the spring.

My own group included Sa-kat, Suk-ee-loon-gawn, the two younger children, Chah-kol, Tu-ma, and the boys' mother, Kee-kee-cheem-wes. We packed our furs and clothes, several round-bottomed clay pots, and as much food from the storage pits as we could carry.

It was a cold, gray day. Chah-kol, leggy and long-armed, took the lead with a bounding stride. He was hardly someone I thought could protect us. All the same, I was glad for his company. We trudged through the snowy wilderness, following the deer trails. Finally we reached the interior of the forest, and the boys built us a makeshift hut of bark and skins.

At night we heard the lonely sound of wolves howling. When one started to howl, others joined in. We had seen their paw marks in the mud at the forest's edge.

The snow piled up outside the hut. As the weeks passed, we ate chestnuts, acorns, and shriveled pumpkin rings. We cooked our supply of dried fish. Then the dried foods were nearly gone. Chah-kol and Tu-ma were not yet expert hunters and seldom came back with anything.

Though Suk-ee-loon-gawn had brought her dyed porcupine quills, we did not do much sewing or decorating. Som-kway once said that if we were angry or fearful or had some other strong negative emotion, we would spoil what we made with our sour feelings. We played counting games with stones. Suk-ee-loon-gawn and I no longer quarreled, and we grew closer in the cold and dark.

Sa-kat and I found ourselves idle until Chah-kol and Tu-ma came staggering in with a plump doe and there were preparations to be made.

Som-kway had said I would one day rely on the customs and traditions she taught me. Now I said all the prayers, songs, and chants that I knew, both in Lenape and in English. My mind went in circles. I tried to have a vision, but none of my spirit animals appeared. The only picture that came to my mind was of a whippoorwill standing on the roof of our long house back in the village. The bird called out three times.

Neither Sa-kat or I could figure out what the whippoorwill's call could mean.

"I wish I could have a vision that could help us," I said.

"We will wait out the winter," Sa-kat said kindly. "Try not to be so discouraged."

"I used to be very proud," I said. "I thought I was different from other people because I had visions. I don't care about that now. Everyone back in the village is suffering, and I have no power to help them."

"There is nothing we can do," she said. "It's the *mah-tan-too-wuk,* the evil spirits. It is the *mah-tan-too-wuk* who make pesky mosquitoes, biting snakes, and illnesses for which there are no cures."

Som-kway had told me that certain bad things, as well as good things, were set in motion like waves. She had also said that it was possible to stop other great ills from happening, waves that had not yet been set in motion.

Then I remembered something else she had said. "You can talk about what is good or bad and deliberate endlessly. In the end, however, you would do best to keep your mind on those great leaders who have journeyed well."

I thought of my mother and Som-kway, two great leaders. What would either of them do at a time like this? Then an answer came to me.

"Sa-kat, we must go back to the village and help Som-kway," I said.

She nodded.

I felt a certain joy at that moment, knowing that I was about to take action. I was not afraid.

Changes

THAT NIGHT I DREAMED I HEARD THE FOOT-
steps of hundreds of spirits walking along the Milky
Way. Sa-kat told me that she'd had the very same
dream.

"It was a vision," I said.

The vision told me that many of the people in Place
of Stringing Beads village had died.

Suk-ee-loon-gawn did not want us traveling back to
the island by ourselves, even though it was only a few
hours' distance. She arranged that Chah-kol would go
with us.

We followed the frozen river. When we reached the
cornfield, I saw the wolf pack. The wolves moved across
the snow in single file with their heads lowered. One
walked in the next wolf's tracks.

"The wolves are at a distance," I said to reassure
myself.

"They won't be bothering us," Sa-kat put in.

I forced myself not to run.

Soon we reached the place on the sound where the
villagers hid a supply of canoes. We dragged a large,

heavy one to the shore. I breathed a sigh of relief when the three of us were safely in the boat.

A layer of heavy fog hung over the black, choppy water. We paddled around chunks of moving ice. Because of the fog, we could not see what lay in front of us. We moved over a large wave as freezing-cold salt spray drenched us. As we turned toward our landing place the water swirled, full of rocks.

An image of a small owl with a white heart-shaped face came into my mind; I saw her flying low over the water. She told me the right way to go through the fog, and I told the others.

Once inside the palisades of the village, Chah-kol ran to find his father, Mah-kwa, and Sa-kat and I headed toward our own long house. Som-kway was not there. The houses of bark and mud seemed oddly empty; I did not see any fires burning. No one walked about, and even the dogs had scattered. The cold wind blew. My clothes were damp. Soon my shivers increased until I was shaking all over. I realized it was from fear as well as from the cold. Where was Som-kway?

Debris of fallen trees, animal bones, and broken pottery lay around us. Two wigwams had blown down in the wind. Everywhere there were signs of neglect. I felt a flash of rage when I realized how quickly the village had fallen apart.

At last I found Som-kway in one of the wigwams, ran to her, and embraced her. She was giving hot herbal potions to the remaining sick people in the village: several children, a middle-aged woman, an older man, and Wam-pak. So Wam-pak had become ill. I took in the horrid smell of urine mixed with the odor of unwashed bodies.

"There were many others who stayed in the village. They have all gone ahead of us to the shadow world," Som-kway said sadly.

The sick people looked at me with bony heads and clear, shining eyes. Their faces looked haunted. I recognized Aleech-kway among the group. I remembered her as a long-legged girl in a dirty dress, running about in a game of tag with the other village children. Now the girl smiled at me and grinned shakily. Her lips were too pale.

I turned to Wam-pak. He stared straight ahead and did not see that I had entered the wigwam. His face was raw in spots. He did not wear any paints on his cheeks. I recognized him only by the mark of the snake on his forehead.

Sa-kat ran over to Wam-pak. *"Noo-ha-tee!"* she called out, "my dear father." She took his hand, and he answered her weakly.

Som-kway herself did not seem well. She had lost weight and her eyes sagged. "My granddaughters, I am glad to see you," she said. "How are Suk-ee-loon-gawn, Mee-kwun, and the baby? Kee-kee-cheem-wes?"

"They are well," I said.

"How are the boys?" Som-kway asked. I could hear the hunger in her voice. She had not had enough food to eat.

"They also are well. Chah-kol is here with us."

"My brother Mah-kwa is still alive," she said. "He is out hunting."

A slight breeze entered into the cracks of the wigwam and broke up the stench a bit. I felt the chill in my bones; the room was freezing cold. The fire was dirty and barely burning. There was food spilled over it and burned into it. Som-kway must be very ill to neglect the fire in this way.

I reached out my hand to steady Som-kway. "*Noo-huma,* my grandmother, you rest now. Sa-kat and Chah-kol and I will look for food."

The three of us set out to find what food was left in the village. Most of the storage pits, already emptied, had been used as temporary resting places to house the dead. We found a few small fish, dried and stiff with their mouths gaping open. They would not be enough. The tide was low at the beach. Though it was far too cold to wade for very long, Sa-kat and I managed to find a few clams. Chah-kol caught some codfish in a net. Back in the wigwam we shucked the clams and roasted them on sticks and boiled the codfish to make a broth.

Mah-kwa returned with a raccoon he had managed to wrest from its burrow. We were so happy to see him! He spoke easily and without alarm. He was not at the same breaking point as Som-kway and the others, per-haps because he had spent time hunting away from the village.

The sun disappeared behind the trees, early. We had a small meal that night; the sick ones were too ill to eat much. The wind blew wildly and the waves moved without stopping. Sa-kat and I returned to our old long house and collapsed into sleep.

News

THE FOLLOWING DAY ONE OF THE SICK children, the little boy about Mee-kwun's age, died. The next was Aleech-kway. I kept her company as her time drew near. She had been a cheerful, simple girl, I remembered. She had lived her life without a thought. Now, in her last breaths, she lifted her small face to me, and I gave her water. After she died, I helped to carry her to one of the outside storage pits. Her body seemed weightless.

Sa-kat and I helped Som-kway make poultices and healing drinks. We filled the sick people's wigwam with the fresh smell of burning cedar. In spite of our best efforts, the sick people died, one by one, all except Wam-pak.

I knew that Wam-pak would live. Even when his lips were drawn and the skin crept on his bones, I could sense the great strength he had underneath. I held a gourd full of broth to his mouth. "Your hair is pretty," he said one day. "I always liked you, Mee-pahk."

About the same time that Wam-pak was well enough to rise from his sleeping platform, Som-kway took ill. Sa-kat and I coaxed her back to our own long house. Som-kway's condition seemed to hold steady, though she slept for most of the day. Som-kway was not able to walk much anymore. I took her hand and pressed it; it was unresponsive. I tried the healing techniques on her that she had taught me. They worked a little.

"When the grandmother and grandfather spirits roll their dice and change the seasons, I want you and Sa-kat to go to my brother Mah-kwa for further training," she told me.

"*Noo-huma*," I said firmly, "we will make you well again." She did not seem to hear me. She slept, and I sat beside her and held her hand to my lips.

It was the first winter I had spent with the Lenape in which there was no storytelling. It was a terrible time. Even Sa-kat was miserable. I missed her merriment. I would lie awake at night and think of my family. It was hard for me to conjure up their faces, but Mother's was not as difficult as the rest. In my mind she was forever sharp, pointed, alert.

By the last snowfall of the season, Wam-pak was well enough to go hunting with Mah-kwa and Chah-kol. They brought back a deer. When the snow melted, we were able to get more food out of storage pits. Suk-ee-loon-gawn, Tu-ma, Kee-kee-cheem-wes, and the little boys returned to the island. About twenty-five others who had fled from the sickness also found their way home. That was all. When I had first come to the island, the village had numbered over a hundred. In the past year it had had fifty inhabitants. Spring had returned, the blue-green marsh grass grew in the flat land near the lagoon, but the village seemed empty and ghostlike. The bodies of the people who had died in the winter were placed in the burial ground off the island. There was talk our village might soon merge with a Wappinger village north of us. Som-kway was better but still very weak.

My monthly cycle started when I was raking the corn hills, preparing them for planting. I held the secret to myself for a few hours until that afternoon, when I told Som-kway. Delighted, Som-kway roused herself from bed, and she and Suk-ee-loon-gawn took me to the beach, stripped me, and dunked me several times in the cold water. I screamed, more from excitement than from shock.

It happened that within a day it was also time for Sa-kat to bleed, so together we slept in the women's hut with a few other girls from the village. Sa-kat and I talked and laughed as we had done in the past, before the sickness. "Nothing much happens, does it?" Sa-kat murmured.

"No," I answered, feeling a small cramping in my stomach. "I don't think there are evil spirits hovering around us. Staying here is just a way to get out of work."

"I'm not sure, but I know Suk-ee-loon-gawn agrees with you," she said.

I decided to bring up another subject that had been on my mind. "You never told me who you were laughing with the night of the flute playing. It was Kee-tak, wasn't it?"

"Yes," she said sadly.

I realized then that Sa-kat loved Kee-tak, and I was sorry he had not returned from the winter. It seemed odd that he hadn't, as his family had left the village when the sickness had first started to spread. They must have died of the pox after all, or the wolves had got them. Or perhaps they had traveled a bit farther away than the others and were just late in returning.

"You cared for Kee-tak, didn't you?"

"Yes," she answered.

I thought of Kee-tak. He was a decent, intelligent, good-humored young man. At one time I had thought his voice was too loud, but I realized now that this had been a petty concern.

A few days later Sa-kat and I returned to the village. Sa-kat noticed a whippoorwill standing on the roof of our long house sometime around sunset. It called out three times. It was the bird I had seen in my vision!

"The call of the whippoorwill means that someone will be leaving us," Som-kway said.

I thought that Som-kway was talking about her own death and begged her to stop. She corrected me, however. She said a whippoorwill meant a departure of some sort; the cry of an owl over the house would have meant a death there.

Sa-kat now seemed more attuned to secret dreams, signs, and portents. "I dreamed of a brown rabbit giving birth to a nestful of babies," she told me one day.

"*Hee-pa-ha!*" I said. "You had a vision." We smiled at each other.

"I think your dream means you will marry soon," I said.

"Perhaps, but the rabbit is one of your spirit animals. I think *you* are that rabbit."

"Our village is so small now. There are few choices for either of us," I answered.

That night, when Sa-kat and I were playing a game with Mee-kwun, a flute player came to the long house and called out Sa-kat's name. "It's Kee-tak!" she said. We both recognized his booming voice. Sa-kat ran out to greet him, carrying a blanket. Hours went by before she returned.

There was plenty of excitement during the next few days. Kee-tak had returned to the island with twenty other family members. Place of Stringing Beads village was not as depleted as we had thought.

I wondered why Wam-pak seemed remarkably somber during this happy time. Then one morning he took me aside. "Messengers have come to our village with word from the chief at the white men's fort. The chief knows you are here. Someone will be coming for you. You are to be traded back to live with the white men."

The Wedding

"I DON'T WANT TO GO BACK!" I SAID.

"You will return to your people," Wam-pak said sternly.

I was stunned. Horrified. Afraid. I wanted to return, and yet I didn't want to go. What would I return to?

"You can't make me leave. I'm going to stay here!" I said.

"Mee-pahk, it is not for you to decide. I have sent a message to the fort. I have agreed to the terms of the leader there. In exchange for you, they will give our village goods and they will not harm us in any way. The Dutch say they will not go to war with us again. You will return to your brother." He showed no emotion.

"My brother? Which brother?" I asked. I thought I would burst.

"I don't know. The man will be waiting for you at the fort."

"When?"

"Before the next moon."

So I would be leaving the village in the summertime, within a month. I was to be sent to the Dutch fort in New Amsterdam. I would go where few, if any, English people lived. Someone would meet me there. Would that person truly be one of my brothers?

Tears welled up behind my eyes. "I don't want to go!"

"I have already made the agreement."

I saw in Wam-pak's eyes perhaps a bit of sympathy, but he would say no more.

The next thing I did was run through the woods to the beach where the Gray Mare stood. I flew into a rage, kicking tree stumps and rocks. I shrieked, alarming the gulls around me. "I hate you, Wam-pak!" I yelled. I blackened my face with ash from an old fire. I was so angry, I did not know what to do with myself. I cursed Wam-pak as I threw stones into the water. Then I climbed up onto the Gray Mare, where I could be alone, to cry. The water spread out before me, a deep blue-green under the shifting clouds. The view seemed particularly beautiful to me at that moment. I loved this place. It was my home more than any home had ever been to me. I would never leave it. Never! I would live on Place of Stringing Beads island until I died.

Before I returned to the village, I washed the soot off my face. I did not want the villagers to know of my trouble. Now was the time, I thought, for Wam-pak to change his mind, before the plans went any further. There was still time for me to save myself!

I finally went to Som-kway, who was resting in her sleeping area, as she now did much of the day. Surely she had heard the news; Wam-pak tended to tell her almost everything. I was glad that I happened to find her alone. I shook her gently to awaken her and sat beside her on the sleeping platform.

"Wam-pak wants me to leave and go to the fort," I said.

"Yes, he told me," she answered. Her strong face seemed more deeply lined than ever.

"I will not go!" I said. "Tell him that I must stay here. He will listen to you."

"Go!" Som-kway said. "We don't need you here!"

I felt as if an arrow had pierced my heart.

Som-kway pulled herself up to a sitting position. She leaned against the wall.

"Don't you want me to stay?" I asked.

"No. Not if it is your time to go."

I couldn't believe what I was hearing from Som-kway, who had taken me in as one of her own.

"I can't go! I'm going to be a great medicine woman like you and help the people of our tribe."

"Sometimes we mistake our ideas for the reality," Som-kway replied.

"Please let me stay. I want to stay," I pleaded. "You need me, especially now that you're ill and so many of our people have died."

"Do you think you're so indispensable?" she asked.

Her words were cruel. I remembered overhearing Som-kway tell Wam-pak that I should be killed for running away. Now, in a few moments, Som-kway had managed to tear down every bit of trust that she had built in me.

I stood up and continued to stare at her, letting the tears run down my face. "Leave me alone! You lied to me," I said. "You made me think you wanted me here, and you knew all along that Wam-pak was going to sell me!"

"Our village is not thriving. You will be better off with your own people," Som-kway said plainly.

"But I want to stay here with you and Sa-kat!"

Som-kway's voice continued to be stern, but all of a sudden it seemed her eyes were kinder.

"Mee-pahk, you are a granddaughter to me. I do not want to see you go. At the same time, I will not argue with an agreement that has been made for the good of our community. When all the Lenape bands came together with the white men to talk about peace, there were many conditions to the treaty. One was that we give up white captives. Perhaps Wam-pak knew about this part of the treaty—perhaps not. But there's nothing we can do now. The Dutch leader knows that you are here."

"I don't want anyone to go to war," I said reluctantly.

I went off by myself in the woods and cried some more. *I must be brave,* I decided. I returned to the long house a few hours later to find Sa-kat serving Som-kway a broth. Sa-kat's eyes were red from crying.

"You can't leave us!" she said. "Wam-pak will change his mind. He won't let this happen!"

There was little time to talk. That night Kee-tak presented gifts to Wam-pak so that he could have Sa-kat for his wife. He gave Wam-pak twenty finely chiseled arrowheads he had made, a cloak of raccoon fur, and a thick belt of purple-and-white *wampum* beads. The next day, in return, Sa-kat cooked a meal of *sa-pan*, corn bread, and dried meat, which Suk-ee-loon-gawn proudly took over to Kee-tak. Suk-ee-loon-gawn returned with word that the meal had been accepted. The marriage agreement had now been sealed.

"I am so happy!" Sa-kat said. She hugged me. Her cheeks were rosy. "But I'm not happy when I think about you leaving the village. We can't let this happen!"

I tried to smile and keep my grief to myself, but my Lenape sister knew me too well. She had never looked as sweet to me as she did at that moment. I discovered how much I loved her.

"Mee-pahk, my little pretty leaf," she said. "We will be together always."

I nodded and was silent. I did not have the heart to disagree.

During the next few days Suk-ee-loon-gawn and Sa-kat readied the long house for Kee-tak's arrival. I watched them move all the baskets in the storage places, sweep the floors, repair a broken pot, clean out the two fire areas, and shift around our sleeping platforms to create more room. I stood apart from everyone as much as I could. The simplest, most ordinary activities of my daily routine could now bring me to tears.

Som-kway roused herself from bed to collect the herbs to make a special bundle. She carved little figures from roots to look like a man and a woman. Then she tied the figures tightly together with sinew. She said as long as the figures remained bound, the marriage would last.

One night Kee-tak's parents and two brothers and sister came with him to our long house and brought gifts of cornmeal and bear fat. We had a larger-than-usual supper that night. But there was no more ceremony than that.

I looked over at Wam-pak, who was dipping his meat in some maple syrup. I thought of how a wolf lies in wait for an unsuspecting deer to walk by. I had been right never to care for him or to trust him. Had he intended to trade me back all along?

I thought again of causes and outcomes. Why it was that now, after three and a half years of captivity, I was going to be traded? Now that I was a Lenape, perhaps my own family members would not want me back. Was Wam-pak truly trading me to avoid future conflicts with the Dutch?

Kee-tak's eyes twinkled as he teased Sa-kat. They sat side by side, eating together. It was easy for him to make her smile. I liked my new brother-in-law. Sa-kat's life lay clear before her now. She'd had a vision. She would be a wise woman as well as a wife and a mother.

But what would my future be?

Som-kway

Nearly a month of waiting passed. Summer came, the season for swimming, digging clams, and paddling in our dugout canoes.

Som-kway grew a little weaker all the time. One day I entered the long house and she was not quite awake. At first she had no idea who was embracing her. She snored gently. Her face had grown narrower. There were soft, bluish circles under her eyes. I listened to her breathing and my own heartbeat quickening. I held her and rocked her, as she had often rocked me.

I brought her some *sa-pan*, hoping she would eat. After a while she sat up in bed, her long white hair loose on her shoulders. When she was awake, her eyes were still sharp. She missed very little. She ate to please me before pushing away the bowl, but I knew she no longer cared to live.

"*Noo-wee-tee*, we are both waiting. I am caught between two worlds, life and death, and you are also caught between two worlds in this life. I will not die until you have prepared yourself to go back to your people."

"I won't go!"

Som-kway's voice had not lost its forcefulness. "You will go with them, and you will walk tall and proud, like the Lenape."

"I will run away in the woods when they come," I replied.

Som-kway sighed. "I will not die until you have prepared yourself to go," she repeated. "I want to see you at peace with yourself. I want our family to be at peace. I do not want to spend any time worrying about you as I walk the path of the stars."

"Then you won't die! I do not want you to die!" I shouted.

"Wam-pak has received another message. The men from the fort will be here in a few days. Your brother will be waiting for you at the fort."

"I don't want to go."

Som-kway and I sat together for what seemed a long time. The doll beings, all newly dressed and fed, sat outside their basket, and their aliveness frightened me.

"Mee-pahk, your task is not easy. You are experiencing the result of many actions. A wave has folded over; it will soon crest and break. You have no choice but to go. Remember that you have many choices, however, within this action. Make the best of all you are given. Also, remember our traditions. They will give you strength and identity. Wrap them like a cloak around you. Use your talent for visions. Listen to your spirit guides. Take care of that snapping turtle of yours, my child."

I saw the snapping turtle in my mind. His eyes were narrow and red. His color looked greenish and gray, his carapace healthy. He was waiting also, but he did not seem distraught. Perhaps he knew something I didn't know.

"Will there ever be peace between our peoples?" I asked.

"I don't know," Som-kway said.

"How can peace be achieved?" I pursued.

Som-kway cleared her throat. "A group of people working together, living by strong, good practices, living mindfully, is what is needed in order not to fall into the evil ways of the *mah-tan-too-wuk*. A joyful group will help you to live mindfully—you have seen this yourself. Around people who are joyful you can mature and grow. If we live mindfully, with support around us, there will be peace."

"What will happen to Place of Stringing Beads village?"

"Perhaps our people will join together to form another village. They will live, though not as they have lived before. My people are a remnant of a prosperous past. As for me, I look forward to meeting my ancestors soon."

"I don't want you to die," I said again.

"We must not be greedy, little one. Our Creator, Kee-shay-lu-moo-kawng, who lives in the twelfth and highest heaven, gives us life. It is a wonderful gift. We must not be greedy for more. It is not part of the agreement that we walk on this earth forever."

I held her tightly and began to cry. She grasped my hand. I remembered other times I had sat with her like that.

"It is not necessary to feel a heavy weight on your shoulders. Be happy for what you have! Now, Mee-pahk, are you ready to go back to your people? Are you ready to go willingly and joyfully?"

"I will go," I said. "But I am afraid."

Som-kway sank down into the bed. "I am very tired now. Tell the others to come in."

I nodded. My heart beat with dread as I stepped out of the long house.

Sa-kat, Wam-pak, Suk-ee-loon-gawn, and the younger children gathered around Som-kway. She breathed heavily. Then she spoke her last words to us: "I'm glad that I was born, that I suffered, and that I will soon walk along the starry path to the land of peace."

I embraced her and pressed my cheek against her cheek. I felt her sliding into the dark. What was it like to die?

Som-kway's stare was fixed upon something before her. She seemed happy. Her mouth was open. She had a remote, waxen look for a moment. Then the life drained out of her face.

She was dead. It was not as strange and terrifying as I had thought. There was a great peace in her.

Mee-kwun began to whimper. Suk-ee-loon-gawn shrieked.

Something had passed from Som-kway to me. What was it? Strength. I felt strength. I felt sadness, but I also felt contentment.

That afternoon and evening Mah-kwa chose four women to prepare Som-kway's body: Suk-ee-loon-gawn, Sa-kat, Kee-kee-cheem-wes, and me.

At first I was afraid to touch her, but I followed Sa-kat's example by rubbing red ochre into Som-kway's cheeks. The red paint would not come off our hands when we were finished.

I felt so shocked and surprised by all that had happened that I began to cry. Sa-kat worked steadily, without fear.

Mah-kwa and Wam-pak and the men danced, and it seemed very strange to me that Som-kway was not there to lead the ceremony. I remembered how Som-kway had thanked the plants and animals and how she had named them all. She loved ceremonies. She would have loved this one.

Suk-ee-loon-gawn boiled dried venison. Toward midnight we brought Som-kway's body out to the center of the village clearing. We blackened our faces with ash from the fire. The chanting began. I joined in with the villagers, though in my shock I found I had forgotten some of the words to the mournful songs. But sound was more important than words, Som-kway once said.

We used Som-kway's full, formal name that day, a name I'd never heard spoken aloud and one we would never speak again: Muh-ka-pa-nooh-kway, Red Dawn Walker Woman.

When it was time to feast, I ate out of respect for the ceremony rather than appetite. A full moon shone directly overhead. Sa-kat was crying. I looked over at her, at her luxuriant black hair and deep black eyes.

On the rising tide the bluefish moved through channels among the sandbars. The full moon would be a good time for fishing, but there would be none that night.

Early the next morning we buried Som-kway at the graveyard on the mainland. Later I took out my canoe. How I would miss it! I thought of Som-kway and tried to move slowly and deeply, enjoying every stroke. The swans circled around me. All at once they took to the air, their necks extended and the tips of their beautiful wings folded down. Dark clouds rolled through the sky and, for a moment, there were silver sheets of rain. Then the sun broke through the clouds.

That night Sa-kat and I walked down to the beach. We washed ourselves in the salty, grayish blue water, which was beginning to cool as the harvesting season approached.

I noticed a school of porpoises jumping in the far distance. "Look!" I said. "Remember when we saw the porpoises together long ago?"

"That was when you first came to us," Sa-kat replied.

"You were always so kind to me. You were the first to accept me."

"I will miss you greatly, Mee-pahk," she said sadly. "I don't know how I will go on to live my life without you."

"You will become a medicine woman of renown, like Som-kway."

"She was truly great," she answered.

"Yes," I said, "and so are you."

Som-kway had once said that great people were the ones who knew in their hearts what to do. "Great people cannot be replaced," she had told me. "They are always present. They continue to shape your life." I knew that something of Som-kway would always live in me, and in Sa-kat as well, the same way I could sense something of my mother in my life every day.

Then I remembered another thing Som-kway had

said about great people. Such people, she said, were like the largest canoes of our village. Not only could they carry themselves across the water, but they could take many others with them. Som-kway was such a person.

The Return

TWO DUTCHMEN WITH CHEERFUL, ROUND FACES arrived in the village one week later, along with their Lenape guide, a very old Wappinger. Wam-pak traded me for three iron axes, an adze and a hoe, a brass kettle, two knives, fishhooks, an empty glass bottle, several handfuls of glass beads—and the promise that there would be no fighting. The Dutchmen would not trade Wam-pak their guns.

The next morning the Dutchmen would take me back to the fort. I was already theirs.

I had prepared myself to leave. I did not participate in the activities of the village, and instead I stood by, an observer once again, with my face as expressionless as Wam-pak's. That night I lay, fearful and agitated, trying to keep the panic down. I woke up suddenly, hours before dawn, my mind already sharp. I wanted to leave as fast as I possibly could. I wanted the day to be over.

The autumn sky was a dull gray. The gulls stood on the shore, as if it might rain. I hoped it would not. If it did, I might have to stay for another day. I could not bear the thought of staying a moment longer.

As the Dutchmen were packing up their things, one of them stared at me, horrified at my bare chest. I had finally begun to develop. "You cannot come to the fort like this!" he said. He took out a long brown dress from his sack and insisted that I put it on.

Shame returned to my life at that moment. When I stepped out from my long house in the dress, I cringed when Suk-ee-loon-gawn and Sa-kat noticed me. I was as ashamed of covering my body with cloth as I had once been ashamed of not covering it. The dress felt tight and itchy. I was not myself without my deerskin skirt.

The journey to the fort would take three days. What was going to happen to me once I was at the fort? Who would meet me? Would it be my oldest brother, Edward? Even before I'd been captured, it had been several years since I'd seen him. Would my family recognize me? Would they want me?

I was relieved that Wam-pak would accompany me part of the distance. Now I truly needed his help.

Sa-kat and I buried Kate, my doll being, that morning. I would no longer be able to dance her. It was a little like watching my own funeral, since I knew I was burying part of myself in that hole.

As the Dutchmen finished assembling their packs and we prepared to go, tears ran down Sa-kat's face. I held back my own tears. She smiled as she put several of her own shell necklaces around my neck, and I saw the joy in her that I loved, her profound sweetness. She helped me to arrange the bundle that would be tied to my back. I kept the little medicine pouch that Som-kway had given me with the charms that would protect me. I carried food and clothes. I wore the bearskin around my shoulders. It was easier to tie it around me than to fit it into my bundle.

Suk-ee-loon-gawn wagged a finger at me in her usual scolding way. *"Woo-lee nee-pa-lee,"* she said, which meant "Stand me up well." She was telling me to stand up straight and tall, have good health, and live a good life in which I would be useful to others. She dragged Es-pun, Raccoon, along beside her. Mee-kwun said good-bye to me, but he was too young to realize that I would not be returning. I looked up from him to Suk-ee-loon-gawn. We gazed at each other a long time before we embraced.

Mah-kwa and his wife, Kee-kee-cheem-wes, bade me farewell, telling the spirits to watch over me. Chah-kol and Tu-ma, returning that morning from trapping beavers, gave me their own good wishes.

Chah-kol started to give a speech. "It has been good to know you, Mee-pahk. We have had difficult seasons in the years we have grown up together. We have had joyful seasons. We all wish at this moment that your time with us were not coming to an end."

Chah-kol was pretending to be a great chief, and I knew someday he would be. But what I desperately wanted was for him to comfort me. I stared at his small, narrow face for a long time, hoping I would always remember the way he looked.

All the villagers I knew best formed a circle around me.

I thought of all the activities I would miss by leaving. In another few months there would be corn, squash, and beans to be harvested, herbs to be collected, a *gamwing* ceremony to be celebrated, fish to be caught before the waters froze.

The two Dutchmen mumbled to each other. "Come, we must leave," Wam-pak said.

I took Sa-kat in my arms and embraced her. I looked at her for the last time.

Then I left with Wam-pak, the Dutchmen, and their Lenape escort. A dozen children from the village followed our party to the western end of the island, where canoes were beached. Here the island was grassy and green right down to the edge.

We took two canoes. I shared a canoe with Wam-pak and one of the Dutchmen. We moved from the shadows of trees into the open bay. Sunlight, breaking through the clouds, gleamed on the water's surface. I sat very still. Then I pushed my paddle down and synchronized my strokes with the motions of the others.

My heart thumped and my breathing quickened. I remembered the first canoe trip that I had taken as a captive. I held back the tears.

The river wound across the lowlands, through tall grasses and swarms of mosquitoes. As we walked, Wam-pak stayed near me. I was glad. In another hour we came to the end of the swamplands, where we hid the canoes in the brush, walked, and then rested as soon as we reached higher ground. I sat down heavily on a stone, for I recognized this land. Somewhere nearby were the graves of my mother and brothers and sisters. *Oh, Mother, I wish you were here to guide me,* I said silently. *I wish you could come with me.*

We walked through mud and grasses, then picked up a winding trail. A large group of black ducks flew up like a storm when we passed. The Dutchmen killed three ducks with their guns. We collected them for our supper that night, though I did not have much of an appetite. Soon we disappeared into heavy cover. We walked in silence. I moved slowly and purposefully, as Som-kway had taught me, and in my mind I could hear her voice, urging me to go on. I practiced being still, even though I felt like screaming and crying and rushing back to Place of Stringing Beads village. I saw nothing but a little bit of sky peering between the leaves and branches.

I'm going to start an entirely new life, I thought. *I don't know what will happen, but I'm going to be happy.*

We slept in the forest under a rough shelter of saplings. The next morning we hiked through rain. The journey seemed to take forever. When would we get to the fort? A panic suddenly seized me. What was going to happen? Was this all a trick? Would I be handed over to Pieter Van Hook?

• • •

The next day's trail led over the hills. From time to time we had occasion to look down from a high place and view the rolling terrain. It was vast and wooded, cut with streams. What would it be like to live in a town again? I remembered tiny shops and narrow houses. At that time a penny had bought a quart of milk or four eggs. Would I remember how to speak English?

I had liked my sisters and brothers. Family. Community. People who knew Mother. My sisters Faith and Bridget. Nieces and nephews. *They are going to like me and I'm going to like them,* I decided. I determined to enter into their world wholeheartedly. That was how I would find happiness.

How old were they now? I was nearly fourteen, so

Edward would now be thirty-four. Faith would be a few years younger than that. Edward had a son and a daughter. What were their names? Elizabeth and Elishua.

We proceeded through the forest, and the views dissolved into a shadowy, wet world. We were small figures walking under the tall, lacy hemlocks. We passed through cold spots in the forest, dark shaded pockets where there were no squirrels or rabbits, no birds chirping, nor any other signs of life.

Hot and tired, we reached the banks of a small river. Wam-pak spoke to the Wappinger guide. I heard him say that after crossing this river, the trail would soon lead to another river, the great North River. There the Dutchmen traded with the Lenape's enemy, the Iroquois. The guide would be safe because he was employed by the white men, but it would not be good for Wam-pak to travel alone in this territory.

I knew, before Wam-pak told me, that he would leave me at this place. For one last time I looked at him, his dark eyes and high cheekbones. His age appeared only in the lines on his brow. As I stood facing him, I was afraid to move. His bald head shone with grease, and the little fringe of hair stood straight up. The snake on his forehead wrinkled a bit as he knitted his brow.

Wam-pak leaned forward as if to say something. I looked deep into his eyes.

I did not hate him. During the past years I had grown close to him in some mysterious way. He was no longer the terrifying warrior chief with the snake face. I saw that he had saved my life. He had been my protector, and he had done much to care for me.

"Good-bye, *noo-ha*," I said. I had never called him Father before, and I would never again be able to call him that.

He looked at me fondly, dropping his stony mask. Then he turned and walked away unhurriedly.

I felt my throat tighten. Until now I had not quite believed I would be left with the Dutchmen. Tears ran down my face.

Now I was completely alone.

New Amsterdam

THE PATH ROSE TO HIGH GROUND. THE RIVER to the west was very wide, slate blue, and still. We came to a wall that extended all the way across Manhattan Island. A gate opened in the wall, and we stepped into the town of New Amsterdam.

We followed the road—Broad Way, it was called—and passed a few farms, then high, narrow houses with pointed roofs. I was amazed by my first glimpse of the townspeople: Dutch girls in long, golden-colored dresses, with white coverings on their heads, hanging out white sheets on a clothesline. They looked at me with disbelief. One pointed to my hair. I suddenly remembered that Dutch and English women covered their heads. Another woman stared at my moccasins.

A Dutchman trotted by on his horse. I stared. A Dutch ship with an enormous mainsail came into view on the river.

I walked unhurriedly, as I had been taught by Somkway. I tried to breathe deeply.

The road passed by rows of small houses, some of wood and brick, others of mud. Everywhere there was activity: horse-drawn carts, people, and cows and sheep and other animals running about untethered. The carts thundered as they raced by. How oddly the men were dressed, with hard, square shoes and pointed hats! The fort, surrounded by a four-pointed wall, stood on the highest ground of the town. A nearby windmill outside the walls turned with the breeze.

Climbing the dusty street, we approached the fort. It was in a state of confusion, the way our village had been after the pox. We passed by builders engaged in repairing the straw roofs of mud houses. Twenty or thirty houses had been damaged recently by fires. Men laid bricks to repair holes in the walls of the fort as well. Pigs jumped in and out of the crumbling walls. A cannon had fallen from its mount and lay on its side. A cock sat on top, crowing.

I longed to see a familiar face.

The Dutchmen led us to a stone house at the center of the fort's courtyard. It had two stories, a pointed roof, small rectangular windows, and a chimney at either side. Beside the entrance of the house grew a fancy garden of trimmed bushes, delicately arranged in circles around other trimmed bushes. I caught sight of myself in a puddle as we walked up the gravel walkway. I felt ugly: unkempt and unwashed.

The outer door opened with a creak as a strange man stepped out. His face was pointed, his nose was long, and he wore his hair in greasy curls. Emerging from under one pantaloon was a silver peg instead of a leg.

He gestured to me to come forward and spoke in a rolling language. He eyed me curiously, with amusement but not disgust. Then he extended his hand to me from underneath a lacy cuff that matched his wide collar. Trembling, I reached out to take his hand. I ventured a quick look at the peg leg.

The Lenape guide translated for me. "This is Governor Pieter Stuyvesant. He welcomes you to his home."

I opened my mouth. I could not speak. I tried to summon my strength.

"The governor says to come inside," the guide translated. "He says your brother is waiting. Your brother is eager to see you."

I pictured a tall man.

We entered a sitting room where several women, one with a baby in her arms, sat on heavy chairs near the fire. My eyes went right toward a man with dark hair seated at a desk. He was writing a letter with a quill pen. He jumped up.

The man was extremely tall and well dressed in a sleeveless jacket and gray breeches. His bright eyes looked out at me from his square, smooth face as he walked toward me with big steps.

I stared down at my moccasins before looking up. I stood very still, facing him.

The stranger's face flushed.

How should I greet this person? He leaned forward and stared at me.

I found myself wanting to go to this man. My father's bright, cheerful look shone out at me from this stranger's face! Like my father, he had a small cleft on his chin and another on his nose. I could imagine something of my own face in him.

"S-Susanna? Susanna Hutchinson?" he stammered.

Finally I nodded.

"I am your brother Edward."

I opened my mouth but no words came out.

"Do you remember me?" my brother asked carefully.

I felt goose bumps form on my arms.

He stared at me in alarm.

"Edward, my oldest brother. I remember you," I said at last. As I spoke, his eyes welled up with tears.

Boston

EDWARD AND I RETURNED TO BOSTON ABOARD a sailing ship, to the house where my parents had once lived. Returning there was like a dream. This was the house that had appeared whenever my mind wandered to my early childhood: large and dark, with a big stone fireplace and an opening that looked up to the sky. How strange not to be in a crowded, smoky long house.

Everyone in Edward's family was so formal! How stiffly they held themselves! I felt that awful sense of not belonging. My parents were gone, my brother had three children now, and no one in this house seemed to recognize me.

When my brother led me through the streets of Boston on our way to the house, people stared at me. It seemed odd to be in a town again with storefronts, hanging signs, dusty streets, horses, and speeding carriages. I was irritated by the noises and the sense of hurry. There were no skinny dogs racing about. There was no drumming. They all covered themselves so completely.

In just these past few days with Edward, my English

was coming back to me. It seemed such a formal language. No one hooted or joked. They hardly laughed.

• • •

On my first morning in Boston, Edward's wife, Catherine, called me to sit down at the table for a meal. I liked her. There was an odor of something sweet about her, the long-forgotten smell of lavender.

My young niece, Anne, who was about four and a half years old, found the courage to emerge from her hiding place near the fire. This had been my old hiding place. She was afraid to meet me because she knew I had lived with Indians. At the table the boy, Elishua, who was six years old, blinked at me furtively. His eight-year-old sister, Elizabeth, ventured a quick look at me. Elizabeth had long, dark hair worn up under her cap, and she had a sweetness that reminded me of Sakat.

My brother uttered a prayer; then Catherine dished out porridge into wooden bowls. Why had we all waited to eat? Why wasn't food put out for the taking?

I watched my hands lifting food to my mouth with a spoon.

There was a heavy cheerfulness to this family.

"Did you sleep well last night?" my brother asked.

"Yes," I said, though I had hardly slept. The bed had felt lumpy. All the furniture in the house was harder and more massive than I'd recalled. I had secretly moved to sleep on the floor, where I woke fitfully, hearing Lenape war cries in my dreams.

I shoved bread into my mouth. When Catherine stared at me, I remembered to chew my food with my mouth closed.

"You don't look the way I'd imagined," Elizabeth said with the truthfulness of a child.

It was a great relief that this child wanted to carry the conversation.

"How did you think I'd look?" I said. I had dressed myself as skillfully as I could in Catherine's frock, but I was brown and muscular. Under the long, tight sleeves my arms were covered with freckles. I hated these clothes.

"I thought you'd have paint on your face. I thought you'd be wearing feathers."

"I did wear paint on my face," I said.

"Elizabeth, please," her mother interjected. "No one appreciates your rudeness."

I decided I liked Elizabeth. She had gumption and personality.

Catherine turned to me. "The children are interested in you," she said with a note of apology. In the morning light her face was kindly.

Edward was leaning back in his chair. He looked striking in the sunlight, I thought. Would I learn to talk to him? Would we like each other? What would be expected of me?

"More porridge?" he asked.

"No, thanks you—no, thank you," I managed. It felt so strange to be speaking in English!

There was the noise of horses clopping by on the street outside. I had forgotten the sound.

"I will buy cloth so that you can make a dress," Edward said. "I hope you will let me know if there is anything else you need."

I looked at him with my face empty. I knew that I had no expression.

It seemed strange to be indoors. The windows were so small that I could not tell what the weather was like outside. I thought of plodding through a cornfield of mud and briary plants, and of the wigwams in Place of Stringing Beads village and how they melted into the dark shades and shapes of the woods. I remembered the gray of the sea. I remembered days filled with so much wind that the trees were constantly in motion. I thought of being in my canoe, relaxing lazily and drifting as the current took me sideways.

Slowly I brought myself back to the conversation. Edward was looking at me with a worried expression. I waited for a feeling of some sort to come to me. I tried to smile.

So far no one had asked me about my life with the Lenape. I guessed that Edward was being polite, restrained. It was easier to talk to his children.

"Your sister Faith will be coming tonight," Edward told me. "She is eager to see you."

"I did not know if she was living or not!" I said. I remembered my oldest sister. She was tall and had a radiant, toothy smile.

"She lives in Boston near the wharves," Catherine said.

"She is married," I recalled. "How many children does she have?"

"Five. She had a baby named Mary just this past June," Catherine answered.

"How about my sister Bridget? Is she still alive as well?" I asked.

"Yes. Bridget lives in Portsmouth, Rhode Island."

"Rhode Island?" I repeated.

"Yes. Narragansett is called Rhode Island now. It is a

colony," Edward explained. "Bridget and her husband, John Sanford, have eight children. I have written to Bridget to tell her you are here. I have also sent word to Samuel, who is now visiting them."

My mind swirled with excitement. I spun around. The cup I was holding fell to the floor and shattered into many small pieces.

"It's quite all right, dear," Catherine said.

• • •

That evening the door was flung open and my sister Faith ran in. "Susanna!" she exclaimed. Grasping my shoulders, she gave me the large, full smile I remembered. Tears came to my eyes as she embraced me. Faith seemed older, quite a bit heavier, too stiff in her long black cloak. Yet I remembered her as if I'd seen her just the day before.

Faith's husband carried their baby into the house. A pack of four children followed close behind. I was confused when I saw them. My glance went from one face to the next. All eyes were on me.

"Faith . . . I am so . . . surprised," I managed to say. My mind raced. Did she miss Mother as I did? Did Faith belong to the same church as my parents had? Did Faith ever have visions?

Faith dropped a tight kiss on my cheek and clutched my arm. The words spilled out. "Thomas Cornell and some other people from the Throckmorton settlement survived the massacre. We met with them and talked to them when they came back to Rhode Island. Thomas Cornell had come to warn Mother about the Indians, but it was too late. He called to you, and he saw you carried off. Your brothers went to the site of Mother's house. They thought you might still be alive, but they couldn't find you. We've been searching for you for years! Come, let me take off my cloak, and we'll sit down together." Her shrill voice reminded me of Mother's voice. How hungry I was for that sound.

Oh, Mother, I thought. *I see something of you in Faith. This long journey was worth it just to hear that voice.*

I blushed because there were so many people around—people I should know. The children clustered together and looked at me with astonishment.

I watched the girls; there was something delicate about the way they held themselves. Their skin was too light. They talked so quickly and loudly that my ears rang and I became agitated.

Faith held my hand. I tried to think of something to say, but it was the Lenape language that kept coming to me. I felt numb, but I tried to think in English. *Pay attention,* Som-kway would have told me.

"My poor dear Susanna," Faith said. "Our world is still very strange to you."

I squeezed my sister's hand.

Faith explained to me that her oldest two sons, along with Edward's son, Elishua, attended the Boston Latin School. Later they would go to Harvard College. "They talk of nothing but becoming merchants with their own sailing ships," she said.

Faith told me about our sister Bridget. Bridget's husband, John Sanford, had become a magistrate in Rhode Island. They owned much land, as well as slaves, oxen, and a ferryboat. Bridget was raising two boys about my own age from her husband's first marriage—his wife had died. Then they'd had six of their own.

I struggled to listen. There was much I would have liked to say to my sister.

"You are brave. Mother would have been so proud of you," Faith told me. "Some still think ill of Mother, but our family is no longer shunned. Did you know that Mother is still famous all over Boston?"

I shook my head.

"Were the Indians terrible to you, dearest?" she asked.

"They were good to me," I said. I looked deep into her eyes. "They were good."

The Three
Mariners Inn

A YEAR PASSED, AND I WAS NEARLY FIFTEEN. The Boston clergymen wanted to interview me, but Edward kept them away. At first I did not often accompany the others to the meetinghouse. When visitors came to the house, I thought about hiding in a space behind the great chimney of the front hall, as I had done as a child. I soon grew to trust that Edward would never allow people to trouble me. I would find my place in this new world. I would feel like myself again.

Time was what I needed more than anything else. I had time, in mild weather, to walk barefoot in the family's farmyard in Braintree, outside Boston. I made my first, clumsy efforts to spin thread again. My young cousin Elizabeth coached me. Together she and I took our lessons in reading and writing. I found I was lacking in many things. I shocked them all, however, in my fearless way of preparing game and tanning skins. When this secret was out, everyone gave me their butchering chores. What did it matter, cutting out a heart or a liver? I was glad to make myself useful.

My sister Bridget came from Rhode Island to meet me. She and Faith treated me like one of their own children, tucking me into bed along with the littlest ones and singing me to sleep so that I wouldn't have nightmares. Catherine scolded me for my appearance a few times but gave me a simply cut dress to wear because I did not like the stiffness of their whalebone bodices. Edward gave me soft rabbit-skin shoes. Sometimes I slept on the floor. I ate my porridge with heaps of maple syrup to remind me of Lenape food. Night after night, near the huge fireplace of my youth, my sisters told me stories, strange stories that were vaguely familiar because they came from my own past. Yet the Indian part of me longed for my Indian family. Sometimes, alone, I chanted the mournful songs I had known.

Everywhere I went, people stared at me. I learned to either avoid their eyes or glare directly into them. They talked too rapidly. But as time passed I grew used to it. I would be strong, as Mother had been strong. I would be as strong as Som-kway.

While picking berries near the family's farm at Braintree, I gave my nieces and nephews lessons in walking like a Lenape. "Move slowly and deeply; enjoy every step you take," I said. I listened to my own words with amazement.

As I became used to crowds of English people, I enjoyed going to the Three Mariners Inn on the wharf with my family. Samuel Cole, the jolly innkeeper, had been one of those who signed a petition to keep Mother in the Bay Colony all those years ago, before Mother had been banished. The tavern was a clean, reputable place, where distinguished visitors stayed whenever they came to Boston. My brother liked to go there to drink ale and find out the news of the week.

On a brisk autumn day I met John Cole, the inn-keeper's son. I had walked down the wide, dirty, leaf-strewn streets and had just entered the inn with Edward when John entered. That day he had taken the afternoon off to fish and had returned to the inn wearing a work shirt, leather coat, and breeches rolled up above his knees. John brought the fresh, clean air of the woods with him, which reminded me of the Lenape.

John walked past me, looked at me, then disappeared into one of the back rooms. In a short time he reappeared, having washed, shaved, and changed into a clean shirt. He went to work, wiping the counter with a cloth. He was handsome, dark-haired, with a well-boned face and clear hazel eyes. His lips were thin and turned up at the corners even when he did not smile.

I looked at him. "I'm John Cole," he said, holding out his hand for me to shake.

John led me to the inn's back room, where women and children were welcome to sit by the fire. Men sat in the front room. When the customers had been attended to, he joined me in the back room. He knew that I was Susanna Hutchinson, the redeemed Indian captive.

The children around me were curious. I related the creation story of the Lenape, how all the world grew from the back of a turtle. John broke into a shy smile when he saw how entranced the children were by my stories. I told them how the Lenape liked to dance and chant. Some days were so hot, I said, we spent all our time in the water swimming—without clothes!

I explained—and they didn't believe me—how medicine women such as Som-kway smoked tobacco. I related how the Indians ate when they liked, and how it was permitted to pull food from the pot at any time of

the day. I talked about Suk-ee-loon-gawn and about Sa-
kat and Chah-kol and Tu-ma.

The Lenape, I explained, liked all weather, even if it
was rain or snow or sleet. This is the way they thought,
I said: What is life offering you now? If it is hot, you
accept that. I told the children what Som-kway had told
me: that you cannot change the waves but you can learn
to maneuver them in your canoe. That no matter how
terrible your surroundings, you can learn to find peace.
That the most perfect things change. That even the
greatness of pain has an end to it. That in the silence
what is truly beautiful will reveal itself.

It was even possible to find a spaciousness in your
heart, I said, when you had been greatly wronged.

As I talked, the room began to fill. Mother spoke to
crowds, I thought. I found that I liked being the center
of attention; I enjoyed being a little different from others and having much to say. I was my mother's daughter.

She would have been proud.

What had Mother valued most of all? Freedom.
Freedom to express herself, freedom to worship, freedom to be unique. Mother had never been able to return to Boston. I think she would have been pleased
that I had, and that my uniqueness was not causing me
trouble. A circle had completed itself.

At the end of the evening John and I sat together on
a bench, away from most people. His cheeks were
flushed and his eyes shone brightly.

I saw that he was more comfortable in his outdoor
clothes than the others were. I saw that he was flustered
and shy, that he had restraint and good manners, and
that he was both gentle and dependable, a simple, hon-

est man. His decisiveness in small acts gave me the feeling that he could push aside large obstacles if he wanted something. I thought he was handsome.

My future passed before me, and I saw that a place for John already existed. I would marry him and have children. I would join in the rhythm of my sisters and my mother before them: conceiving, bearing, feeding children. I saw myself singing to my babies the Lenape songs that Som-kway had taught me. One day John would hear me singing to the children in a strange language and he would be angry. In the end he would learn to accept it.

The night was drawing to a close, and my brother had come into the room to bring me home.

John Cole gave me a shy look.

"Are you coming back to the inn? Perhaps tomorrow?" he asked.

"Yes," I said. "I believe I will."

Historical Notes

THE REAL-LIFE SUSANNA HUTCHINSON WAS born in November 1633 in Alford, England, to famous colonial rebel Anne Marbury Hutchinson and William Hutchinson, a merchant. Susanna was the youngest daughter and second-youngest child of fifteen (three died before she was born).

The Hutchinson family were Puritans, people who broke apart from the established Church of England. In 1634, when Susanna was one year old, the Hutchinsons, seeking religious freedom, emigrated to Boston in the Massachusetts Bay Colony. In leaving their homeland, the Hutchinsons became part of a great migration abroad that had begun with the *Mayflower* to Plymouth Colony in 1620. Between 1620 and 1643 about twenty thousand men, women, and children left England for the New England colonies.

Soon after the Hutchinson family settled in Boston, Anne Hutchinson incurred the wrath of the powerful Puritan clergy by challenging their authority. One of her arguments was that every man and woman, not just the clergy, could know and interpret the will of God. She accused the clergymen of teaching people about rules, or "forms," rather than divine forgiveness, or "grace." A prominent midwife with many friends in the community, she broke the traditional silent role of a colonial woman by holding public meetings at her home to give her own views on the sermons of the

Boston church. Unfortunately for her, her house stood across the street from that of her rival, Governor John Winthrop, who kept a close eye on her activities.

In 1637 Governor Winthrop and the Boston clergy brought Anne Hutchinson to trial for preaching false-hoods (heresy) and for disturbing the peace. In a fiery courtroom scene she further angered the church au-thorities by claiming to have visions in which God talked directly to her, expressing His disapproval of the clergymen. Governor Winthrop said she was "a woman of haughty and fierce carriage, of nimble and active spirit and a very voluble tongue, more bold than a man." Winthrop found her guilty but decided to delay banishing her from the colony because it was winter. After he had held her prisoner in the home of one of his relatives for four months, he brought her to trial a second time. She was finally banished from the Massa-chusetts Bay Colony in March 1638. As soon as the snow melted that spring, the Hutchinson family and followers moved to Narragansett, later known as Rhode Island.

The Hutchinsons and their group purchased the is-land of Aquidneck, now part of Rhode Island, from the Narragansett Indians, with the help of Roger Williams, another famous colonial personality, who himself had been banished from Massachusetts. Their settlement, rough dwellings made at first from holes in the ground, was Rhode Island's first town, Portsmouth. A second town, Newport, soon followed.

Anne Hutchinson and her youngest children stayed in Portsmouth for about five years before moving to the Dutch territory of New Netherland (later New York State). Historians speculate that she had a variety of reasons for leaving Narragansett. There were political problems within Narragansett related to the governing of the towns. Larger political problems involved the Massachusetts Bay Colony's threat to take over Narragansett (which did not yet have its own charter to become a colony). In 1642 William Hutchinson suddenly died.

The following year Anne Hutchinson, her six youngest children, a married daughter, Anne, and son-in-law, Reverend William Collins, moved to the Dutch wilderness territory. They probably spent no more than two seasons settling their farm near Long Island Sound (the exact location is believed to be what is now Co-op City in the Bronx, New York City), when in the late summer or early fall of 1643 the family was massacred by Indians. The sole survivor of the massacre was nine-year-old Susanna Hutchinson, who was taken captive.

When they moved to their new home, the Hutchinsons were probably not aware that the Dutch and the local Lenape Indian groups were fighting. The conflict is now known as Governor Kieft's War. In February of 1643 the Dutch, under the command of their governor, Willem Kieft, slaughtered about five hundred Lenape men, women, and children in Pavonia (Hackensack, New Jersey) and Corlear's Hook (on Manhattan Island) in a bloody, unprovoked attack. Afterward Governor Kieft negotiated a temporary peace, which was not accepted by the Lenape. By that fall all the Lenape bands on both sides of the Hudson River, western Long Island, Westchester, and southern Connecticut went on the warpath, plundering, burning farms, and killing all the white settlers they could find.

It is not known exactly which group of Indians captured Susanna or where she was taken. She may have been with one of the Westchester or Connecticut Lenape bands, the Siwanoy or Wiechquaeskeck. The Lenape were an Algonquian-speaking people who later became known as the Delaware Indians. More than a century later the Reverend Robert Bolton recorded that an Indian warrior named Wampage had killed Anne Hutchinson and her family. Bolton says he adopted the name of Annhook. According to Bolton and various other sources—which, after an exhaustive search, I could not substantiate with original documents—Susanna was held captive for two, four, or six years before she was traded back to unnamed friends or family members as part of a peace treaty between the Indians and the Dutch.

Susanna married John Cole on December 30, 1651, at the age of eighteen. He was about nine years older. John was the son of Samuel Cole, who had the first inn in Boston, the Three Mariners. This tavern was on the west side of Merchants Row, midway between State Street and Faneuil Hall. Susanna and her husband moved from Boston to Kings Town, Rhode Island, sometime before 1667 to look after 661 acres owned by Susanna's brother Edward. John Cole became a town magistrate.

Susanna bore eleven children: Samuel, Mary, John (who died young), Anne, a second John, Hannah, William, Francis, Elizabeth, Elisha, and Susanna. At least half of these children lived to adulthood. John Cole died in 1707. Susanna died sometime between 1707 and 1713, between the ages of sixty-four and seventy.

The notable descendants of the Anne Marbury Hutchinson family (descended from Susanna, her brother Edward, or her sisters Faith and Bridget) include Thomas Heyward, signer of the Declaration of Independence; John Singleton Copley, artist; James Abram Garfield, U.S. president; Alfred Iréné du Pont and Henry Belin du Pont, industrialists; Franklin Delano Roosevelt, U.S. president; Oliver Wendell Holmes, poet and essayist; William Averell Harriman, governor of New York; Benjamin David "Benny" Goodman, orchestra leader; Louis Stanton Auchincloss, novelist; and George Herbert Walker Bush, U.S. president.

• • •

The descendants of Wampage in lower Westchester had lived in the region for many hundreds of years. By the 1600s they were reduced to a fraction of their original numbers, decimated by smallpox and other diseases brought by Europeans and also weakened by warfare with the Dutch. The newly emerging colonial society forced small bands to move and gather in the center of Westchester. They crossed the Hudson River to join the Lenape of New Jersey. Some went on to Pennsylvania and Ohio. By the late seventeenth century a great migration had begun that would lead them ultimately to reservations in Oklahoma, Wisconsin, and Ontario, where several groups of the modern-day Delaware Nation live today.

Though efforts have been made to accurately depict the customs of the Lenape Indians in this book, artistic liberties have been taken. Where discrepancies exist, the responsibility is mine alone. The *gamwing* or Big House ceremony and the doll dance were important religious rites among the Lenape of the late historical era, but little has been written concerning these spiritual practices at the time of European contact. However, it is likely that these ceremonies existed long before they were recorded.

A note about the language: It was virtually impossible to accurately represent the gutturals and other sounds of the Lenape language in English. Many of the Lenape words have been simplified for the reader. At least several dialects of Lenape were originally spoken throughout the traditional homeland. The dialect in the lower Westchester region that the Siwanoy would have spoken is known as Munsee; however, for ease of reading I have also used words from the closely related Unami dialect.

All the Indian characters, aside from Wampage (Wam-pak), are fictitious. *(Wapahkw*—probably pronounced "Wampahkw" in some dialects of southeastern New York and western Connecticut—is the closest real Lenape word I could find.) All the white characters in the book are real people. Documentation about the Puritans was available, while documentation about the Indians was not. Some of the place names are derived from names in historical documents; others were created. The word *Lenape-haw-king,* used to describe the Lenape homeland, was created in the 1970s by Nora Thompson Dean, one of the last full-blooded Lenape Indians. The names *Lap-ha-wah-king* (Laphawaxking, Place of Stringing Beads) and *Uk-wa-nu-may-wung* (Àkwanumewàng, Aquehung, or Aque-on-ounk, Place Where They Fish with Nets) appear on old maps of the region in relation to the Bronx River rather than the Hutchinson River; and the Island of Shells, translated into the Lenape form *Cheek-wu-lu-lee-shing*

(Chikwàlàlishing, or Place of Seashells), is an old name for City Island.

Today much of the setting of this book remains parkland within Pelham Bay Park, in Bronx County, New York City, and one of the major routes to this park is the Hutchinson River Parkway, named for Anne Hutchinson. It runs through lower Westchester County and the Bronx, with views of the small Hutchinson River, partly paved over by the parkway, and passes by Co-op City, where Anne Hutchinson's farm is believed to have been located. Within Pelham Bay Park, visitors are welcome to see the woods and beaches described in the book, as well as local landmarks such as Mishow Rock and the Gray Mare. The island where I situated Place of Stringing Beads village in the book is Hunter Island, now no longer an island but joined to Orchard Beach's parking lot by landfill.

Lenape words

Both Munsee and Unami forms were used in this list.

PRONUNCIATION KEY

a	as in English h<u>o</u>t
à	as in English b<u>u</u>t
e	as in English h<u>a</u>te
è	as in English b<u>e</u>t
ë	as in English kill '<u>em</u>
i	as in English m<u>ee</u>t
ì	as in English <u>i</u>t
o	as in English n<u>o</u>te
ò	as in English s<u>a</u>w
u	as in English boot
x	similar to German guttural *ch*
w	at the end of a word, as in *m<u>a</u>xkw*, "bear," is voiceless

An underlined letter signifies stress

Form used in book	Correct form	Translation
a-lup-see!	al<u>à</u>psi!	hurry
ans-ha	<u>a</u>ns'ha	dip it up
cheet-kwu-see!	chitkw<u>ë</u>si!	be quiet! shut up!
eh-chay!	ech<u>e</u>!	*exclamation when surprised*
eh-chay-tam-way!	ech<u>e</u> t<u>a</u>mwe!	*exclamation when very surprised*

Form used in book	Correct form	Translation
gamwing	ga̱mwing	Big House
ha!	ha!	*exclamation of laughter*
he!	he!	hello, hi
hee-pa-ha!	hi̱paha!	*exclamation of joy*
hoo!	hu!	*exclamation of joy*
hum-mee!	xa̱mi!	feed me!
ka-yah!	kaya̱!	*exclamation*
ku-la-mah-pee!	këla̱mahpi!	behave
Kee-shay-lu-mee-eng	Kishelëmi̱eng	Creator—*when addressing God (vocative)*
Kee-shay-lu-moo-kawng	Kishelëmu̱kòng	Our Creator, *literally* one who thought us all into being
koo	ku	no
kook-hoos-uk	ku̱khu̱sàk	owls *(pl)*
mah-tan-too-wuk	mahtantu̱wàk	evil spirits

233

Form used in book	Correct form	Translation
ma-nu-too	manẽtu	spirit
ma-nu-too-wuk	manëtuwàk	spirits (plural)
mee-mun-dut	mimẽndët	baby (boy or girl)
meet-see!	mitsi!	eat
mah-kwa	maxkw	bear
mu-sha-kay!	mëshake!	sit down (on the ground)
Mu-sing	Mësìngw	Living Solid Face
mu-teh-kway	mëtèxkwe	medicine woman
nee-chan	nichan	my daughter
noo-ha	nuxa	father (vocative)
noo-ha-tee	nuxati	dear father
noo-huma	nuhëma	grandmother (vocative)
noo-la-mul-see	nulamàlsi	I am well
nooh-wee-tee	nuxwiti	my grandchild (vocative)
oh-tas	ohtas	doll being

Form used in book	Correct form	Translation
pam-boo-tes	pambutis	snapping turtle
pa-pa-hes	papaxès	redheaded woodpecker
pa-lee-ah!	palia!	get away, *as in* go away!
pah-see-aw-tum	pàhsiòtàm	half-wit
pet-hak-hoo-way-ok	Pèthakhuweyok	thunder beings
peel-seet	pilsit	pure, *literally* one who is pure
sa-pan	sapan	corn mush
say-hay!	sehe!	*exclamation*
shu-wa-nuk-kooh-kway	shëwanàkuxkwe (female)	white person, salt person
tak-ta-nee	taktani	I don't know
wew-too-na-wes	wèwtunëwès	merman
wem-ah-tay-ku-nees-uk	wèmahtekënisàk	wood dwarves, all-over-the-woods creatures *(pl)*

Form used in book	Correct form	Translation
wing-gay-oh-kwet	wingeòhkwèt	raven, one who eats meat
woo-lee nee-pa-lee	wëli nipali	stand me up well, *i.e., live a good life, be of use to others*
yooh!	yuh!	yes! *(reply to a question or statement that can be answered by English "okay" or "all right")*
yoo-ho!	yuho!	yes! *(emphatic)*

CHARACTERS' NAMES

Form used in book	Correct form	Translation
Aleech-kway *(short for* Wap-aleeh-kway)	Wapalixkwe	White Corn Tassel Woman
Chah-kol	Chahkol	Frog
Kaw-kwu-lu-pek-ooh-kway	Kòkwëlëppèkuxkwe	Turning Water Woman

Form used in book	Correct form	Translation
Kee-kee-cheem-wes	Kikichịmwis	Wood Duck
Kee-tak (short for Keeh-kee-tak-see)	Kixkitạkwsi	He is heard nearby
Kwu-nu-moohk	Kwënàmuxkw	Otter
Mah-kwa	Mạxkw	Bear
Mee-kwun	Mịkwën	Feather
Mee-mun-dut	Mimẹndët	Baby
Mee-pahk (short for Nin-gu-mee-pah-kee-now)	Nìngëmipahkịnao	Pretty Leaf, she who appears as a pretty leaf
Muh-ka-pa-nooh-kway	Màxkapanụxkwe	Red Dawn Woman
Mu-teh-kway	Mëtẹxkwe	Medicine Woman
Noo-chee-kway (short for Noo-chee-hu-weh-kway)	Nuchihëwẹxkwe	Witch Woman
Nee-ka-na-pa-nooh-way	Nikanapanụxwe	One Who Walks Before Dawn

Form used in book	Correct form	Translation
Sa-kat (short for Sa-ka-ta-eh-kway)	Sakataèxkwe	Emerging Flower Woman
See-pu-neh-kway	Sipënèxkwe	Water Lily Woman
Som-kway	Somxkwe	Great Woman
Suk-ah-sun	Sëkahsën	Black Rock (usually refers to iron or steel)
Suk-ee-loon-gawn (short for Suk-ee-loon-gawn-eh-kway)	Sëkilungònèxkwe	Black Wing Woman
Siwanoy/Sha-wa-no-wuk	Shawànowàk	Southern People
Tu-ma (short for Tu-ma-kway-lundj)	Tëmakwelëndj	Beaver Hand
Wam-pak	Wampahkw or Wapahkw	Chestnut Tree, White Tree
Wap-akun-eh-hing	Wapakànèxing	White Antler

PLACE NAMES

A-mee-mee-ha-king	Amimimhaking	Place of Pigeons
Cheek-wu-lu-lee-shing	Chikwàlàlishing	Place of Seashells
Eh-hus-sing	Èhësing	Place of Clams
Ha-kee-ha-kun	Hakihakàn	Cornfield *(or garden)*
Ka-ak-ha-king	Kaakhaking	Geese Land
Kita-heekun	Kitahikàn	Ocean
Ktu-mak-su-wa-king	Ktëmaksëwaking	Pitiful Place *(burial ground)*
Kwee-kweeng-ha-king	Kwikwinghaking	Place Where There Are Ducks
Lap-ha-wah-king	Laphawaxking	Place of Stringing Beads
Lenape-haw-king	Lënapehòking	Place of the People
Mus-kay-kung	Màskekùng	Place Where There Is a Swamp

Mus-kay-kwee-ming	Màskekwiming	Place of Swamp Huckleberries
Nee-sha-mu-na-tay	Nishamënatai	Two Islands
Su-ka-nah-king	Sëkanaxking	Black Treetop Place
Tah-koh-ee-mu-nu-pek	Tahkoximënëpèk	Turtle Pond
Uk-wa-nu-may-wung	Àkwanumewàng	Place Where They Fish with Nets

Bibliography

Bolton, Reginald Pelham. *Indian Life of Long Ago in the City of New York.* Port Washington, New York: I. I. Friedman, 1971.

————— *A Woman Misunderstood: Anne, Wife of William Hutchinson.* New York: Schoen Printing Company, 1931.

————— *The History of the Several Towns, Manors and Patents of the County of Westchester from Its First Settlement.* New York: J. J. Cass, 1905.

Dean, Nora Thompson. *Lenape Indian Cooking with Touching Leaves Woman.* Dewey, Oklahoma: Touching Leaves Indian Crafts, 1991.

————— *Lenape Language Lessons.* Dewey, Oklahoma: Touching Leaves Indian Crafts, 1979.

Harrington, M. R. *The Indians of New Jersey—Dickon Among the Lenapes.* New Brunswick, New Jersey: Rutgers University Press, 1963.

————— *Religion and Ceremonies of the Lenape,* Indian Notes and Monographs: A Series of Publications Relating to the American Aborigines. New York: Museum of the American Indian, Heye Foundation, 1921.

Hults, Dorothy Niebrugge. *New Amsterdam Days and Ways: The Dutch Settlers of New York.* New York: Harcourt, Brace, and World, 1963.

Kraft, Herbert C. *The Lenape: Archaeology, History, and Ethnography*. Newark, New Jersey: New Jersey Historical Society, 1986.

———— *The Lenape or Delaware Indians: The Original People of New Jersey, Southeastern New York State, Eastern Pennsylvania, Northern Delaware and Parts of Western Connecticut*. South Orange, New Jersey: Seton Hall University Museum, 1996.

Kraft, Herbert C., and John T. Kraft. *The Indians of Lenapehoking*. South Orange, New Jersey: Seton Hall University Museum, 1985.

McGovern, Ann. *If You Lived in Colonial Times*. New York: Four Winds Press, 1966.

Morgan, Edmund S. *The Puritan Family: Religion and Domestic Relations in Seventeenth-century New England*. New York: Harper and Row, 1944 (reprinted 1966).

O'Callaghan, E. B. *History of New Netherland Under the Dutch*. 2 vols. Philadelphia: G. S. Appleton, 1846–1848.

Oestreicher, David M. "The Munsee and Northern Unami Today: A Study of Traditional Ways at Moraviantown," in Herbert C. Kraft, ed., *The Archaeology and Ethnohistory of the Lower Hudson Valley and Neighboring Regions: Essays in Honor of Louis A. Brennan*, Occasional Publications in Northeastern Anthropology, no. 11. Bethlehem, Connecticut: Archaeological Services, 1991.

———— *In Search of the Lenape: The Delaware Indians Past and Present*. Scarsdale, New York: Scarsdale Historical Society, 1995.

Rugg, Winnifred King. *Unafraid: A Life of Anne Hutchinson.* Boston and New York: Houghton Mifflin, 1930.

Ultan, Lloyd. *The Bronx in the Frontier Era: From the Beginning to 1696.* Dubuque, Iowa: Kendall/Hunt, 1993.

Waheenee. *Buffalo Bird Woman's Garden: Agriculture of the Hidatsa Indians,* as told to Gilbert L. Wilson. St. Paul, Minnesota: Minnesota Historical Society Press, 1987

Williams, Selma R. *Divine Rebel: The Life of Anne Marbury Hutchinson.* New York: Holt, Rinehart and Winston, 1981.

Winthrop, John, *Winthrop's Journal: "History of New England" 1630–1649,* edited by James Kendall Hosmer. New York: Charles Scribner's Sons, 1908.

Acknowledgments

WHEN I FIRST READ A NEWSPAPER ARTICLE
that mentioned how Anne Hutchinson's daughter was
captured by Indians, and I thought to write a novel on
the subject, I had no idea of the amount of research
that would be involved or the help I would need to
complete the project. The three-year journey would include listening to Lenape language tapes and auditing a
college course in archaeology, reading Dutch documents in translation, finding old maps, and hiking and
kayaking through the area. Every step of the way I was
helped by new acquaintances and friends found during
the course of the project, who provided ideas, sugges-
tions, materials, and referrals.

In particular I would like to thank Dr. Herbert C.
Kraft for his longtime work in the field of anthropology
and archaeology, for his encouragement, teaching, and
generous use of research materials, and for reviewing
the manuscript. I am deeply indebted to linguist and
Lenape scholar and friend Dr. David M. Oestreicher for
helping me with the Lenape words and names in the
book, as well as for telling me stories of the Lenape
medicine woman Nora Thompson Dean—including
the merman, the Silent Walker, and the doll beings—
that became part of this story. Jim Rementer, a Lenape-
speaker and member of the Delaware Nation, provided
David M. Oestreicher with some of the linguistic infor-
mation used in the book. I alone am responsible for

liberties taken with the material and any errors. I thank my friend Jorge Santiago for providing me with old maps of the Pelham Bay area as well as many articles and books. The staff of Touching Leaves Indian Crafts provided books, Nora Thompson Dean's language tapes, and other invaluable materials; it is my hope that this book will be helpful in furthering the wishes of Nora Thompson Dean and other Lenape traditionalists who wanted their culture preserved. I am also indebted to the many others who have helped me with historical research: Mimi Buckley and the staff of the Pelham Historical Society; Nancy Fischer; the staff of the Heye Foundation; Mary Lou Hallatt; Fred Lane; Joan Leland and the staff of the New England Historic Genealogical Society; John McNamara and the staff of the Bronx Historical Society; the staff of the New Rochelle Public Library; Neil Steinberg and the staff of the New York Public Library–City Island Branch; Susan Swanson; Bill Twomey; Carolyn Freeman Travers and the staff of Plimoth Plantation; the staff of Ward Pound Ridge Reservation; and Eric Wessman.

I would like to acknowledge Wendy Lamb, my editor at Bantam Doubleday Dell, who guided this project with sensitivity, and my literary agent, Dorothy Markinko, of McIntosh and Otis, who also believed in this book.

I am grateful to Marianne Fuenmayor and Susan Ji-on Postal, two wise women teachers of the heart, for their words and ideas. Many meetings and life experiences I have had in the past few years crept into this book; things that were said to me in entirely different contexts appear in the character Som-kway's conversations. In some cases I have drawn Som-kway's teachings from Native American sources, in other cases from the Zen tradition; yet I believe that the philosophies are often in keeping with each other.

The members of my writers' group offered generous support, valuable critiques, inspiration, and friendships: Stephanie Cowell, Peggy Harrington, Ruth Henderson, Isabelle Holland, Casey Kelly, Judith Lindbergh, and Elsa Rael; thanks to Sanna Stanley, and a special acknowledgment is due to Jane Gardner, who read every draft. Thanks to my beloved mentor, Madeleine L'Engle, the focal point of our large and vibrant writers' community, which now numbers more than a hundred members. I am grateful to Mary Veronica Amison, Renée Vera Cafiero, Mary Cresse, David Edwards, Thea Hunter, Shirley Litwak, Elizabeth Peréz Ode, Daria Rydzaj, Marcia Savin, Sheri Seifert, and Kira Schachinger, who suggested revisions or provided other editorial assistance. Thanks to John Griffiths and his fifth-grade class at the Siwanoy School in Pelham, New York, who also read this book in manuscript form. Others have contributed in a number of important ways: my family, Audrey and Dale Kirkpatrick, Sidney Kirkpatrick, Jennifer Kirkpatrick-Zicht, and Eric Zicht; Roberta Racianello; and Jonathan F. Tait.

About the Author

KATHERINE KIRKPATRICK lives on City Island, in the Bronx, New York City, a few miles from where Anne Hutchinson's farm once stood. As part of the research for the book, she enjoyed kayaking around the area. City Island was the setting for her first novel, *Keeping the Good Light,* winner of the New York State Marine Education Association's Herman Melville Book Award and a New York Public Library Book for the Teen Age.

She grew up in Stony Brook, Long Island, New York, and graduated from the Stony Brook School and Smith College.